WEST COUNTY

A JEFF TAYLOR MYSTERY

The Jeff Taylor Mysteries
by Scott Lipanovich

The Lost Coast

The Golden Ceiling

Sky Lake

West County

WEST COUNTY

A JEFF TAYLOR MYSTERY

Scott Lipanovich

Encircle Publications
Farmington, Maine, U.S.A.

Cover design by Christopher Wait
Cover painting: "West County" by Don Bishop

Editor: Cynthia Brackett-Vincent
Book design by Deirdre Wait

Encircle Omada

Published by
Encircle Publications
PO Box 187
Farmington, ME 04938

info@encirclepub.com
http://encirclepub.com

For Hannah and Nat; Nat and Hannah:
Thank you for giving me a second, richer life.

"I firmly believe, from what I have seen,
this is the chosen spot of all this earth
as far as nature is concerned."
—Luther Burbank, legendary horticulturalist

PART ONE

One

Spring came early to Sonoma County, and nature threw a party. Each plant and tree hastened to rise from the earth and claim its share of paradise. I'd never seen as many shades of green. The bright greens at the tips of new growth were downright intoxicating. It was my first spring in the region; I was dazzled. Everywhere I walked, everywhere I drove, brought feelings of endless possibilities, of good things to come.

Two hummingbirds flitted, branch to branch, wings purring. Tiny green torsos sparkled under crisp sunlight. A red spot shone at each throat. The birds hovered on adjacent branches of a mature lilac bush. A hushing wind joined the birds' purring. It occurred to me it was possible they might not be hummingbirds, that to untrained eyes they could be little creatures that looked like hummingbirds. Living in a region that was profoundly fecund, of late I'd realized how little I knew about the natural world. Did that mean I knew little about life?

I did know that where I stood held magic: SunSpot, a secluded nature preserve seventy miles north of the Golden Gate Bridge, three miles in from the sea. I viewed distant, tree-covered ridges, the mouth of Tomales Bay, and Point Reyes National Seashore. Cream-colored clouds with silver bellies drifted slowly landward like ships floating in the sky. Directly ahead of me a large garden, ornamentals and vegetables, curled down a hillside, out of view.

Upon checking my phone, it showed that ten minutes had passed. I walked to the center of a grass field. "Bianca! I give up. You can come out now."

Bianca Vasquez, nine years old. She liked to see how long she could keep me searching in games of Hide and Seek. I hadn't searched at all. It was more fun to stroll upper grounds at SunSpot and take in the landscape.

"Bianca! You win. Come on out."

I checked the usual hiding places on the preserve's mesa-like hub. Around the corners of wood buildings gray from years of drenching fog alternating with sunshine. The garden. The rectangular greenhouse. A communal kitchen/eating area that was open to the land at one end.

"It's time to go," I called out. "We have to head back."

Bianca, a strong runner, could cover a lot of ground in ten minutes. She'd been out of sight for more than fifteen.

"Bianca!" A hint of desperation seeped into my voice. "Come on out. It's time to go home."

I jogged across the grass to a bench placed where a trail began, a looping trail that went up and then down a green hillside. Behind the bench, wild grass grew tall. Tall enough for someone as diminutive as Bianca to hide in.

"Bianca!"

Every Saturday I watched Bianca from noon until four, giving

Inez, her mom, some free hours. Inez was Executive Director of the public health clinic where I worked, and my lover. Yates Health was a mostly free provider, situated half a block off the one commercial street in Yates, population about a thousand. On weekends that number rose substantially. People drove through forests and lilting grasslands, past vineyards and small farms to procure favored treats, to have brunch or beer and a sandwich at outdoor tables. The town was a stripe of paved land that ran between towering redwood trees.

No Bianca behind the bench, though two juvenile lizards, riding the thick damp grass, legs churning like paddle wheels, fled. I turned around, looked to the greenhouse. A more thorough greenhouse search was all I could think of to do.

"I got lost!" Bianca's shout came from behind me. "It was an adventure!"

Telling myself to not let any alarm show, I turned and walked to her. Bianca's cheeks were bright with excitement. Curly dark brown hair covered half of her face. Her breathing signaled she'd been running. Bianca wore a navy-blue T-shirt with a circle of dolphins on its front, jeans with holes at the knees, and red tennis shoes. Her nose turned up a smidgen at its tip.

"What kind of an adventure?"

I met Bianca as she reached the plateau. We slapped five, our customary greeting. I used my left hand, as my right is without the two smallest fingers, and half its middle finger, the result of a work accident seventeen years prior.

"I got lost," Bianca said. "A teacher lady helped me!"

"A teacher lady? Why call her that?"

"Because she was. I went down to sneak over and hide in the

3

garden. I got lost. A teacher lady came." Bianca's voice fizzed with delight. "She said, 'Follow me.' I did. Then she said, 'Your turn to go first. Don't stop till it gets flat.'"

"There wasn't a car for a hiker. I wonder where she came from."

Bianca's dark eyes danced. "When I got in front and turned around, she'd disappeared!"

We walked across the green field. "I'd like to thank her, but the chances of finding someone down there are almost zero. Too many trails."

We passed the elaborate garden. Bianca stopped. She shook her head. Her whole frame wiggled. "She's not a real hiker. She wore a dress. She didn't even have shoes on."

I gently patted the top of Bianca's head. "Let's get some ice cream on the way home."

Bianca looked up. I rarely bought treats. She'd learned not to ask for them. "For real? No joke?"

"Ice cream is not something we joke about. It'll be kind of to thank that person for helping you."

Bianca hustled toward my brown Subaru. She shouted, "She was weird but nice!"

"Hey. Don't talk like that. It's not okay."

Bianca stopped, looked to the ground, and slowly shook her head in contrition. "Can we still get ice cream?"

After dropping Bianca at her and her mom's house in the small city of Appleton, I headed south on semi rural Highway 116 in search of a dining table. Since taking the clinic job, I'd eaten at a scarred coffee table, while seated on a brown couch, staring at my laptop. I'd delayed buying many furnishings until certain I'd stay. My track record of staying at a job was not exemplary. Yates Health was the third in five years. The road changed from two lanes each way to one. At the edge of town were cafés and shops that gave way to gas stations and burger joints, auto repair businesses, a tire shop, and a few antique stores. Between these were small apple and almond orchards. Below the almond trees, white petals littered the ground like confetti.

I pulled onto the paved area in front of a large wood structure. The building's walls were reddish brown, with ODIN'S ANTIQUES painted above the entrance in large letters the color of butter. Jammed inside were old furnishings, dusty paintings and various oddities. A four-sided counter sat in the middle of the large, high-ceilinged space. Beneath it were glass compartments stocked with collectibles. The place smelled vaguely of mildew.

Odin, six feet, sturdy, about fifty, stood behind the counter. I'd first met him at one of my Sunday dinners, taken at Homer's Café in downtown Appleton. Homer's was the kind of place where strangers struck up conversations. Today Odin wore a straw hat, jeans and a gray sweatshirt with MICHIGAN LACROSSE printed across its front in blocky, dark blue letters. He haggled with a young couple regarding the price of a reclaimed stained-glass window.

I meandered through tight lanes of items more suited to the phrase second-hand than the word antique. I came upon a trio of dining tables, including a substantial French farm table. None were the better for wear. I overheard the couple at the counter say goodbyes. I knew Odin not only from Homer's Café but also from buying an end table and lamp to set beside the brown couch in the converted garage that was my home. Odin clicked open the counter door, exited and clicked it shut behind him. He walked toward me and lifted his straw hat in greeting like cowboys do in old movies. Odin's voice landed with a Scandinavian accent.

"The farm table is a bargain. Got it at an estate sale, at the Dolcini ranch outside Petaluma. They're one of the old dairy families."

"No thanks." I looked at the table and realized it wasn't so bad. "You know, maybe I can't find one that seems good enough because I used to have one I loved. It was teak. Solid as hell."

Odin's pale face and hazel eyes conveyed cheerful bemusement. His mouth seemed to have too many white teeth. "Teak? As you say here in the U.S., that's right in my backyard."

"You mean it's right up your alley."

Odin shrugged, and slipped a phone from his jeans. He produced an image of a golden-brown teak dining table. Odin placed the phone in my undamaged left hand.

"I have a second store," he said. "Sort of a West County annex. By appointment only." Odin caught sight of a woman stepping to the four-sided wood counter. She set two ceramic pots on it. "Flip through the pictures," Odin said. "Come find me when you're ready to buy."

Another toothy smile; he'd spoken in jest.

The table was a thick slab of teak. The grain lines were prominent. Polished but not slick-looking, it seemed suitable for meals as well as for a work desk. The customer concluded her purchase. Toting a green pot in each hand, she walked out. I went to the wood counter and gave Odin his phone.

He set it down, stepped sideways, and folded arms across his chest. "Well?"

"How much?"

The price seemed fair. "I want a ten percent discount. Like with the lamp and end table."

"Already factored in."

"Why should I believe you?"

"Why shouldn't you?"

"Go fifty dollars less and I'll think about it."

"One condition," Odin said. "Cash sale."

"Your taxes are none of my business," I said.

"I'm closed here Monday through Wednesday. That's when I spend time with my wife, and take private appointments." He moved forward, one-two long steps. Odin shook my hand like we'd just concluded a considerable transaction. "Give me your email." He snatched his phone and turned it face up. "I'll forward the pictures."

I gave my email address, and added, "Like I said, I'll think about it."

When I left, Odin lifted his hat. I didn't have the heart to tell him American cowboys didn't salute people with a flimsy straw hat.

Sunday morning, I drove west with the intention of jogging at Dutton Beach. In my head I heard Bianca say, "She didn't even have shoes on."

A small percentage of patients who came to Yates Health

were homeless. Some were unstable. Bianca's Teacher Lady was quite possibly both, and likely living off the power grid. It wouldn't be difficult to hide on three hundred unspoiled acres. Challenges included getting enough to eat, staying warm, and perhaps staying on an emotionally even keel. It seemed wise to check on her.

Quail skittered in front of my Subaru as it rolled down the unmarked dirt road leading to SunSpot. A red-tailed hawk circled above, scouting breakfast. A white SUV rested in the parking area. Heading into the preserve I took in the view of the ocean and Point Reyes, crossed the grassy flat area and started down the trail Bianca had returned on. Smells of fresh plant growth came from every direction.

A mile later the trail curved right and up, looping back toward the bench where I'd looked to see if Bianca had been hiding behind it. I started in that direction—and a feeling of being watched landed on my shoulders. I halted. Far below, redwood trees grew in a valley damp enough year-round for them to thrive. Searching the ground, I made out what I'd normally think was a deer path, and followed it.

In morning shade I walked down what became a steep hill. The grass damper than in the sunlit beginning, it made dark spots on the cuffs of my jeans. At an opening in the vegetation was a newish-looking steel mesh fence, five feet high. On it were two signs.

PRIVATE PROPERTY
NO TRESPASSING

And:

NO HUNTING
SONOMA CTY ORD. 30458

Past the signs, rightward along the fence, in green-leafed coyote bushes were glints of steel. Looking the other way, the same, until a dark space in the brush. Beyond the dark space, more glints of steel.

The coyote bushes were too dense for me to work my way along the fence. I walked a half circle, scoured the landscape and found a low opening. Below my waist there was a tunnel in the brush. I crawled in, and passed an opening in the fence with No Trespassing and Wildlife Corridor signs secured at one end. A trail dropped to a grove of magnificent redwood trees. The scent of the trees' fallen detritus was potent. Again I felt watched.

I'd grown up in a redwood forest; it felt like coming home. I walked downhill, into those dark woods. At the base of a massive specimen, mostly out of sight, a blue tarp was hitched onto chunky, sorrel-colored bark. I looked around at trees that sprouted before Columbus set sail for the Americas. Sounds of creaking branches came from above. I walked to the tarp.

"I'm not here to bother you. I'm here to thank you for helping my friend's daughter yesterday." I spoke louder. "I'm also here to make sure you're okay."

Not surprisingly, no response.

"I don't think you're in there, but I'm going to open the tarp. To make sure you're okay. Okay?"

I stepped forward, grabbed the top of the tarp, unhitched it and pulled it to the right like drawing open a curtain. A low entrance was framed by blackish charred bark, undoubtedly the result of an old lightning strike. Inside was a warren, the tilted ground made level by a bed of redwood duff packed in like mulch. The duff was covered with two tan blankets. Along the perimeter of space about the size of a child's fort were small boxes, folders, jars and flowers, all neatly organized. I re-hung the blue tarp, made sure it was wedged firmly in the sturdy bark, and left.

Two

Shannon Lunge had a standing appointment, first Monday of the month, before he went to whatever house he would paint that day. No matter the weather or season, he wore a white T-shirt. Five feet ten, 230 pounds, Shannon had the stoutest jowls and most drooping double chin I'd ever witnessed. It was as if he'd been pumped full of air from the neck up. I worried he'd someday explode. Shannon's receding brown hair ran through a rubber band, giving him a short ponytail. Crimson splotches were scattered across his face.

Sitting on the examining table, Shannon said, "Why you don't give me 'em for like three months a pop?"

I watched numbers as the blood pressure cuff tightened. "You get the blue pills for almost nothing. I get to keep an eye on your health. And make sure you're not overdoing it with Viagra."

"I have needs, Doc. I have significant needs."

"Try to relax."

Shannon closed his eyes and sighed in what was apparently his way of attempting to relax.

"You're fifty-one, right?"

"Since January."

"Do you take your meds consistently?"

"Both of 'em." The cuff now removed, Shannon shook out his arm. "What're my numbers? I'll use 'em for lotto."

"One forty-nine over ninety-five."

Shannon's splotchy red face pulled together in surprise. "I've been exercising like you said. Walking and hitting the weights."

"How about we get you some exercise after work? Five-thirty? If you'll take me to Burnside Road, you'll get fifty bucks for putting a table in your truck and taking it to my place in Appleton. Take you an hour and a half."

Shannon said, "Fifty? More like seventy." He laughed hoarsely. "Just kidding. I'm in."

"To give fair warning, if you've been drinking, I'll call the sheriff's office and have them get a deputy to follow you home. I don't think you can afford another DUI."

Shannon hopped off the examining table. "It's under control, man. See you later."

Shannon was only ten minutes late. He'd put on a fresh white T-shirt. He wiped crumbs from his mouth as I climbed into a faded blue pickup. It reeked of soaked-in cigarette smoke and stale beer.

I said, "Do you know Moonlight Road, off Burnside?"

"Give me the address, we're there."

Shannon wielded an aggressive, insistent attitude. The ends of his T-shirt sleeves were rolled up to show ample biceps. He talked fast, drove fast, and seemed uncomfortable with any lapse in conversation.

Leaving downtown Yates, the road swayed back and forth

through redwoods. The pickup groaned and screeched. We entered a valley of grasslands, crossed it, climbed into forest and snaked our way to Moonlight Road. At 4142 Moonlight, Shannon cranked the steering wheel left. We ascended an asphalt driveway that leveled off. Ahead was a three-car garage painted the same reddish-brown as the outside of Odin's antique store. To our right loomed a two-story wood house of the same color. Its front door swung inward. Odin emerged and skipped down redwood steps with potted plants to both sides. He lifted his straw hat. I lowered the window and said hello.

"I assumed you have a truck," Odin said. "You should've told me." He looked in at Shannon rather than at me. "We could have worked it out."

Shannon said, "Where do I park?"

Odin hesitated, then said, "Go left, and back around to the center door."

Odin walked to that center garage door. He used an automatic opener. Tires squealing, Shannon maneuvered the truck into place. Unlike at the antiques store, where he was easy going, chatty, Odin hurried and said little. He hardly looked at Shannon and me as he asked for help moving a few items aside. Everything in the oversized garage was high quality. Paintings were dust-free and nicely framed. On the back wall a metal-framed business license shined under lights.

The three of us got the table into the bed of Shannon's pickup. Shannon knew ropes. As he tied down the table I handed Odin an envelope with money inside. He said thanks and goodbye and scooted back into the garage. I figured he had another customer coming.

The sky had softened. Shannon exited the driveway, turned right and flicked on headlights. Tires crunched gravel. Shannon shook his head. He laughed and smacked the steering wheel. "You don't even get it."

"Don't get what?"

"Most the merch in there was hot. Prices were too good."

"Didn't you see the business license? It's legit."

Shannon's large head turned toward me like the stone head of an Easter Island statue. "Why keep it hidden out here, unless it's stolen? You see how nervous he was about me showing up?"

"You can be intimidating to someone who doesn't know you. I think you're aware of that."

Shannon snorted, shook his head again and turned left onto Burnside Road, already dark under tall trees lining asphalt. The pickup bounced and squeaked. Within a turn the road dropped abruptly. Shannon fought the turn. Tires howled.

"Slow down. Watch the road."

"Woodrow," Shannon said.

The pavement leveled off. Shannon sped up again.

"Hey, Woodrow," I said. "Why don't you slow down? I'd like to make it home in one piece."

"Woodrow's not a name."

"Then what's it mean?"

"Depends on the situation."

"I don't get it."

Shannon squeezed the steering wheel. "You're a college boy. You'll figure it out."

Three

Mid-week, before heading out for work, I stocked my day pack with food that didn't need refrigeration. In an envelope was a note: *Jeff Taylor, M.D., Yates Health*. Below that, my phone number and *Call any time, for any reason*. At the clinic I'd learned it wasn't especially unusual for a homeless person to have a cell phone. It couldn't hurt to leave a potential way to make contact in an emergency.

Bianca's Teacher Lady walking barefoot in the wild added to my thinking that she wasn't operating on all cylinders. The first thing to do was assist with items she'd need. The idea was to build trust.

At work a patient who needed considerable attention showed up as the doors were being closed. By the time I reached SunSpot, the sun, half a yellow ball, swam in the ocean.

No trouble remembering the way. I crawled through the thicket tunnel, the wildlife corridor opening that would have been mandated by the county when the steel fence was installed. Already dark in the cathedral-like redwoods, the air was cooler there than when coming down the hill. In gloaming light, the blue tarp shone dimly. I called out a hello, announced I was dropping off food, and that I'd then leave.

I unhooked the tarp, went to my knees and entered the teepee-shaped space. I slipped off the daypack. The tan blankets appeared brown in the meager light. A botanical drawing of grasses and tiny wildflowers, nicely rendered, sat on a low cardboard box. I'd been in the tents of many unhoused people and had never seen anything as squeaky clean as that tree abode. The food and envelope with a note in it were set on the blankets. Sitting up I lost my balance in the soft mulch, fell forward and stopped myself with both hands pushing into the spongy floor. My lips skimmed the edge of a thin blanket. Serenity spread throughout my body. It seemed I'd touched something blessed. I grabbed the empty day pack, backed out on my knees. Outside, the air was cold again. The peaceful feeling evaporated. I put on the pack, re-attached the blue tarp. The redwood bark felt good against my hands.

Winding my way through primordial trees, I was moved by what had transpired in the hut, when my lips skimmed the blanket. I felt I'd touched something magical. Walking uphill toward the opening in the fence, noisy rustling sounds advanced toward me. Teacher Lady?

A dozen feet away, a California black bear appeared. Its mouth made a sputtering sound. I locked eyes with several hundred pounds of wild animal. What happened next was the bear's choice. I had no influence over an outcome. The behemoth's sputtering hisses terrified me.

Clapping sounds came from down the hillside. Over and over, closing in quickly, came the incessant quick-loud clapping. The bear turned toward the sounds. Its right foreleg rose in what I thought was the beginning of the bear standing.

"Be off with you." The voice, clearly female, was of no discernible age. It sounded firm, not anxious, and certainly not frightened. "Be off! You go away. Now."

The loud clapping grew nearer. The bear lumbered off, crashing through brush. I saw shadowy bushes, nothing more.

The person I assumed was Bianca's Teacher Lady said, "Everything is okay."

Heartbeats slammed my chest and throat. Dizziness caused my hands to reach out to both sides, as if I might fall.

"Thank you," the woman said, "for all you brought." She sounded nearby, yet somehow, also far away.

"No problem."

"I'm here a lot longer than I expected. I keep waiting."

Silence. I didn't hear anything move.

Finally, Teacher Lady said, "What would be appreciated is a set of drawing pencils, and good drawing paper. Thank you for listening to this request."

I looked into the shadows, trying to locate her shape. "What is it you're waiting for?"

"I never know. But if you tell people I'm here, it won't happen. I won't be able to do it."

"I won't tell anyone."

"You should go before the bear comes back. It won't harm me. Thank you again for what you brought."

I scurried uphill and through the thicket tunnel, and hiked up the path with the aid of my phone's light. By the time I crossed the plateau and SunSpot buildings, all fear had departed from within. Once inside the car, I worked off the daypack, turned on the engine and headlights to help orient me. I looked in the rear-view mirror, and watched my lips move.

"Did that really happen?"

It had happened. Who was Teacher Lady? How did she effortlessly scare off the bear?

Halfway home, my phone sang. Slowing on the unlighted road, no one behind me, I took my phone from a front jeans pocket. Odin.

He spoke in a high-pitched, artificial nonchalance. "There's been sort of an accident."

A push of a button and emergency blinkers came on. I slowed down the car. "What happened?"

"Too hard to describe over the phone. I'm asking for your help."

"What kind of help?"

"I'm asking you to come over. As in quick. I'll pay."

"You need to tell me what happened."

"Soon as you get here. You're coming, right? Come in the front door. How long will it take from where you are?"

"A guess is twenty minutes. Are you experiencing pain? Should you call 9-1-1?"

"Just hurry."

Odin clicked off.

West County people were known for their independent streaks. Odin fit the mold. Was it fear or impatience that animated his voice? During the drive to Odin's house, replaying his voice in my head, I decided it was fear. This caused me to hurry up to see what had spooked him.

The areas in front of Odin's house and garage were brightly lit by spotlights attached to the garage eaves. I parked close to the steps, snagged the black doctor's bag that traveled everywhere with me from the backseat. I hurried up redwood stairs past the potted plants, knocked on the wood door, stepped into the entryway.

"Over here. In the dining room."

I followed Odin's voice through a doorway, past a sink on one side, a high-end gas range on the other. Sprawled on a floor of ginger-colored tiles, Odin was in front of a dining table and chairs. A towel under his upper right arm and shoulder, his phone within reach, blood soaked through the towel and oozed darkly onto tile. I went to the floor, snapped open the doctor's bag and took out scissors designed to cut adhesive tape.

"What the hell happened?"

Odin squinted. He wasn't wearing the straw hat. Hair still blonde above the ears, he had a bald pate. This made the protruding white teeth appear even more prominent. He looked a dozen years older than the evening I'd bought the table from him.

"I asked you what happened."

"Well, I guess I kind of got grazed."

"You mean shot? What I see is somewhere between grazed and shot."

"I'll be fine."

Sitting on my knees, I cut away his shirt where blood was. "Self-inflicted?" The shirt's shoulder and sleeve were set aside.

Odin shook his head. His exhales grew louder. I applied a temporary bandage over a slice two inches long and a quarter inch deep. Doing this relaxed me in the same way it always relaxed me to work on a patient. The focus kept the mind from straying into avoidable mental inquiries.

"I'm going to give you some Lidocaine to numb this. Then check to be sure there isn't anything foreign in there."

I administered the shot.

"Let's give this a couple minutes."

I went to the sink and washed my hands. This was the first abnormal phone call I'd ever received from a patient, the first that crept into illegality. Looking outside I saw the lighted asphalt area with plenty of room between the house and big garage. Trees were trimmed so as not to block the view of hills rolling toward the Pacific Ocean. I filled two glasses with tap water, and returned to Odin. He drank some, set the glass aside. I did the same, and went to work cleaning the wound. Next I sewed in eleven stitches. The whole time, including a final cleaning and applying a full-on protective bandage, Odin craned his neck to stare at the top of his arm. Most people would look away. Others, like Odin, seemed to revel in seeing their bodies damaged.

He sat up, put his left hand to the tile floor, and clamped his teeth. He was going to stand. I didn't let him.

"We'll sit here a bit more. Let things slow down." I grabbed Odin's glass of water, and handed it to him. "Have some more. Your voice is dry."

"I'll be fine."

"That's right," I said. "By the way, where's your wife? You know, who you spend time with Monday through Wednesday, when you're not taking appointments."

After buying the dining table for cash, and Shannon's

20

insistence it was stolen, I'd searched Odin De Laat online. Found nothing other than a listing for the antique store, though I did find entries for his wife, Crystal Bench, with Odin listed as her spouse. An actress, she'd starred in cable TV shows in her teenage years and later landed bit parts in movies. Now in her forties, she had a recurring role in a soap opera.

Odin said, "My wife just got a gig in an upcoming family series. They're calling it "Potholes." It's for some streaming platform nobody's ever heard of."

"So she didn't shoot you?"

"Crystal's in LA."

"By law I'm supposed to report this to the police. Give me the person's name. I won't ask questions."

Odin sat up, then sank back onto tile. "It was a misunderstanding. And you don't want these people to know *your* name."

I shook my head. "A bullet passed through you. Period. You said people?"

"Two." Odin's words sped up. "I'm not protecting them. I'm protecting us. Will three hundred cover things? And keep it quiet?"

"I'll help you get up, to see if you can walk to your bedroom. Put a towel under your wound. You'll be okay. Out of the antique business for a while, but okay."

Odin reached for a back pocket with his left hand and fumbled for his wallet.

"I can't take it, because I was never here."

"I owe you one."

"You can't owe me one because I wasn't here. Make sure you drink plenty of water. Eat something, even if you feel nauseous.

And don't put any weight on that arm. You'll tear the stitches. I'll check on them in a week. Now, let's get you on your feet."

Odin didn't need help.

I shut my black bag. The leftovers of cut shirt and bandage and blood were Odin's to deal with. "Will your wife be here next Wednesday, say six o'clock?"

"She comes home this Friday."

"Make up a good story, because I'll come by in a week to be sure this is healing okay. Your store stays closed. Order a sling online. It'll stop you from tearing out the stitches. And don't let any shower water get under the bandage. As in none."

Odin followed me through the kitchen to the front door. He was durable. He opened the door and shook my half of a right hand with his left. "I still say I owe you one."

"Say it again, I'll report what happened here."

I left gladly. In eight months I'd made lots of house calls for Yates Health. I volunteered for them because it was a good way to learn about the area. And house calls were usually interesting. They helped me see into a patient's life. None had been as interesting, or as disturbing, as that one.

Four

An April Fool's Day rain made a nattering sound on the roof. The rain increased into a wonderful downpour. Eleven in the morning, Inez's bed moaned as if expressing its own expanding delight. She arched her back and spilled my name into a room flooded with the scent of burning lavender candles. Inez's flesh was warm and moist. Mouth buried in the crook of her neck, her taste accompanied the sensations thrilling me down below. I withdrew, went to her dresser and extracted a shiny black velour scarf.

"Is that for me, or you?"

"It's to make us one."

Inez's eyes closely followed my movements. I set the springy scarf on the bed, then draped it from her throat to between her legs. I lengthened Inez's arms overhead, glided the bottom end of the scarf up her smooth nakedness and reached with my arms. I bound our wrists together, two of hers, one of mine, and cinched them tight in a double slip knot.

I steered myself home. Our bellies meshed, parted, meshed. We recommenced the sacred dance. My feet curled around Inez's ankles; I desired every inch of her. Inez's hips went crazy.

My hips went crazy. A pounding, like drumbeats, rose from the bed as the headboard smacked the wall. Our skin grew slick.

We went at each other instinctively, irrationally. Inez's dark hair flew like she'd been thrown from a whirling helicopter. We slammed into each other ever faster. Her body clenched and she shrieked. White lights exploded in my head. My body convulsed. Inez called my name, this time faintly.

I panted like an animal after running for its life. Inez's moans were an erotic chant. The flashing lights in my head gradually dispersed. For a time, I couldn't think straight.

"Good god," I got out. "Jesus."

We rolled onto our sides, facing each other. Wrists bound above our heads, stretching the velour scarf, our cheeks brushed each other's. I licked Inez's sweat, freed us from the scarf. We went onto our backs. The ceiling seemed alarmingly close.

"Whatever this is," Inez said, "I hope it doesn't kill us."

My half-hand went to her damp brown hair. Words came out slurred, like I was drunk. "There're wo-worse ways to go."

"Let's not talk about it. We might jinx it."

We drifted in separate return trips. Everything appeared ultra clear. Dresser drawers had gained new distinctiveness. The colors of ceramics gleamed as if lighted from within. Beyond a short hallway, and the living room, the front door opened with a loud scrape of old warped wood. We popped up. I reached for my walking shorts and sweatshirt and looked for my socks.

Inez said, "*Crap.* Bianca's way early."

I hurried into the one bathroom and ran cold water at full blast into the sink, for noise, while slipping on my clothes. I splashed water on my face, told myself to slow down, to not allow Bianca to see anything unusual in my facial expression.

Bianca called out, "I'm home!"

She'd be unlacing tennis shoes, then placing them in a low wood box next to her mom's and mine.

Inez somehow pulled herself together, got her clothes on and made her way down the hallway. "Hey there. Was it fun?"

On Saturdays the Appleton High School gym was open to elementary school students from nine until noon, when I'd then take Bianca on an excursion. Kids from all over West County converged and played informal games, some indoors, some outdoors. Inez did the drop off. The mother of Bianca's best friend Ellen picked up. Bianca was home a full hour early. I flushed the toilet and joined them, slapping Bianca a high five.

She wore a bright blue Golden State Warriors T-shirt, the letters gold, and jeans. Water marks dotted the T-shirt; a few raindrops nestled in her hair. Bianca chewed gum and bounced a red rubber ball on the wood floor. Inez told her to stop. Bianca looked at us like she knew something was up but had no idea what that something was.

As a diversion I took the red ball from Bianca's hands. "This isn't a basketball. What do you play with it?"

"I'm third grade wall ball champ, including boys."

"Don't boast," Inez said.

"You always say tell the truth. I'm third grade wall ball champ. We use the outside gym wall. I couldn't play today because of the rain."

I handed the little ball to Inez. "Could you hold this? Miss Truth and I have some furniture to rearrange."

Bianca and I emptied the dining room of three birch chairs and a potted Ficus. We dragged the small eating table against a wall. This left one obstruction, a weaving of what I'd been told was a Golden-fronted Woodpecker. The weaving was tacked onto the wall. It had belonged to Inez's grandmother, in Guadalajara. I asked Bianca if she had any chalk. A minute later, a minute during which Inez assured me that if her grandmother's weaving were damaged I would experience a slow, tortuous death, I had a stick of green chalk in hand. I went to the longest wall—the walls were wood—and drew a line about thirty inches above the floor. The ball could touch the line. If ball hit wall above the line, it was out of bounds.

"I've clearly lost my mind," Inez said. Her hands squeezed the top of her head. "Why am I allowing this?"

"Because you love me!" Bianca said.

"No. It's because you two have a *game* to play. Go ahead, wreck the house. Play your stupid game."

We took off our socks and played barefoot.

Mid-battle, Bianca claimed, "In!"

"Out," I said. "By at least three inches."

"Do over. I get a do over."

"Ine." This was my nickname for Inez, *nine* pronounced without the first *n*. "Wasn't that out? It didn't touch the line. Hey, you're supposed to be the referee."

Inez sat in the adjacent living room. She flipped a newspaper page. Lean from the waist up, strong as a draft horse from there down, Inez's dark skin, reflecting a mix of native Mexican and Spanish heritage, gave her an old-soul appearance. Her clothes were consistently one or another hue of brown.

"If you want my input," Inez said, "I say let's work on the Yosemite puzzle. We're not even half done."

Bianca said, "Nobody's ever allowed to have fun here. *Ever.*"

The game was to twenty-one, like ping pong, and like in ping pong you had to win by two points. When we reached twenty to twenty, we took a break. Bianca paced, tugging at the ends of her dark hair. Puffing, I stretched out on the floor. Inez came over. She dropped a towel on my face.

"Today's workout a little too much for you?"

I dried my face and said, "Let's go."

Bianca won, twenty-six to twenty-four. I conceded defeat, and said it was time to go to the Children's Learning Center, in Santa Rosa.

"Be right back!" Bianca raced to her bedroom. Inez and I were in the kitchen. We heard Bianca chattering on her cell phone, which came equipped with a tracking device, a godsend for single parents.

I washed up at the kitchen sink.

Inez wrapped an arm around my waist. "Thanks for letting her win."

"The hell I did. I demand that kid be tested for steroids."

Inez said, "I saw you let up a few times." Tears came quickly to the inside corners of her eyes. Inez turned away. "I don't want to be like this. Not after you two had so much fun. But it's hard. She sees her dad like every six weeks. When she does, they spend half the time at his girlfriend's parents' house."

I looked toward the hall, spoke in a low voice. "We should be more careful with Bianca."

Inez whispered, "If she came in even five minutes sooner,

we would've been nailed. Ellen's mom has never been early like this."

"You really do it for me," I whispered.

Inez kissed me. "You're not so bad yourself."

Five

The kitchen at Yates Health was the only large space remaining in a chopped-into-offices, century-old Grange Hall. A staff meeting was held there every other Monday morning at seven-thirty. Heated bagels and blueberry cream cheese, and a thin-crusted vegetarian pizza sat on a counter of worn Douglas fir boards. A pot of lemon grass tea. Food smells joined the smell of old wood walls and floors, and six tables that were ten feet long. We gathered around one, ate and talked.

Besides Inez and me, there was Gerald "Storm" Elliot, M.D. Forty-five years old, of average height and build, Storm moved with a calculated swagger. He rode a growling Harley Davidson. His black leather jackets—he sported a few—had slits here and there, like battle scars.

Storm's opposite in temperament and style was Sandy Lewis, M.D. In her early sixties, with short light-brown hair, she was an enthusiast on the kind of cycle powered by human legs. Sandy was slim as a pike, clear-eyed and unassuming. Gray eyes set off a face that while showing her years, radiated fine health.

Youngest was twenty-seven-years-old office manager Robin Mengee. Robin functioned as a kind of air traffic controller for the clinic, overseeing day-to-day operations. She'd started as a volunteer after graduating from high school. She worked retail for a few years, didn't much enjoy it, and jumped at a chance to return to Yates Health when the office manager position opened up. Recently divorced, Robin had two pre-school boys in day care.

Finally, Suzanne Bradshaw, physician's assistant. She wore big, red-framed glasses that made her dark eyes appear enormous. Black, she had an Afro that raised her to six feet. She walked tall and had a commanding speaking voice.

Informal catch-up conversations went on until Inez pointed the index finger of her right hand upward, thereby calling the meeting to order. Emailing an agenda had probably never crossed her mind.

Inez said, "I spent yesterday going over the books with Morrison." Harvey Morrison did the clinic's books for free. "To be honest, I'm not sure we'll make it through the year. Calendar year, not fiscal."

Sandy gazed straight ahead. "No offense, but when you're overworked you tend to say this."

"She's always overworked," Storm said.

Sandy glanced at him. "Maybe that's why she says these things so often."

My thought: *Here we go again.*

"I for one would like to see hard figures," Storm said. "In fact, I think I have a right to." His eyes swept the table. "We all do."

Suzanne's toothy smile squelched Storm's bluster. "The day this sister starts handing out charts is the day I know we're in real trouble. You don't appreciate how fluid Inez is. How much she juggles just to keep the lights on."

Storm shook his head. As usual during staff meetings, I didn't offer an opinion. I still felt like the newcomer who had to prove himself. Sandy looked to Inez, trying to gauge the moment. Robin's eyes were filmy. Her options for a good job elsewhere were limited.

Inez's hands went up, then lowered in a kind of benediction. "Enough jousting. Here's what you need to know. During the pandemic—even after—we operated high on money flowing from the Feds. We were able to stash some, but those days are long gone. I've been beating the bushes to supplement the old pandemic money, with little success."

Storm said, "How much are we talking about? How much a month are we short?"

"Eight thousand, give or take."

Storm scoffed. "Give or take? That doesn't sound like generally accepted accounting practices to me."

"Because we juggle," Suzanne said. Her dark eyes gleamed. "You want to be like everybody else? We need money? Let's get a winery to pay an annual fee to slap its name on the side of the building. Let's get a license to sell beer and wine on the front porch."

"I'm not against some kind of sponsorship," Sandy said. "But I don't think a winery would be appropriate."

Storm said, "I assume this means no cost-of-living adjustment."

The talk droned on. I wondered what Teacher Lady was doing, alone on three hundred pristine acres. I pictured the stately redwoods, and remembered how deeply at home I felt there.

"Well," Inez said, "speaking of salaries, I'm taking a five percent cut as of May first. Part of my strategy with potential supporters is to show our commitment."

I looked to my colleagues. "I'm okay with that."

"Of course you are," Storm said. "The rest of us don't have a wealthy ex. Who by California community property law has to give you half of everything when you settle."

The room fell as silent as the redwood grove I'd been daydreaming about.

"You don't know what you're talking about," I said. "And it's none of your business."

"Prenup?"

Storm looked across the table as if challenging me to repeat it was none of his business. His face, usually pale, was pinkish and seemed swollen. It was pleasurable to watch Storm make a fool of himself.

"No prenup. Maybe you've heard of this. We trust each other to be fair."

Inez snapped, "That's enough. Nobody's going to be forced to take a pay cut."

Chin knifing the air, Storm nodded to everyone individually. "No pay cut here." Scraping his chair backwards, he stood and puffed out his chest. Storm's motorcycle boots sounded a march across the wood floor. "If you'll excuse me, I have work to do."

The boot sounds faded. At the end of the hall, a door shut loudly. Suzanne got up, carefully closed the kitchen door, and snickered. Everyone joined in though the decibel level was kept low. In my short stint at Yates Health, this was the third time Storm had left a staff meeting in a huff.

Inez snatched a remaining chunk of bagel. "Tomorrow's D.D. will have a piece in it about the clinic." This meant the *Daily Democrat*, Sonoma County's dominant newspaper. "It'll tell the clinic's history. The article will describe our situation. Let's hope it attracts an angel to keep us open until I can scare up more institutional funding."

Robin stared at her hands, folded, resting on the table. She hadn't spoken since money matters were introduced into the conversation.

Inez looked to Robin. "You don't have to explain yourself."

"That's right," I said. "You're feeding three on one modest salary."

Suzanne sent me a sly smile. Did she suspect Inez and I were lovers?

Sandy said, "I'm in, but only 'til the end of the year."

"Same here," Suzanne said.

Robin's face looked like she was about to apologize for not being able to contribute.

Inez didn't give her a chance. "Now that that's settled," she said, "let's finalize everyone's schedules for May. I'll email Storm for his."

Six

On Wednesday I called Odin and said it was time to check on his arm. "I expect you to be wearing a sling. You tear out those stitches, we have to start over."

"I'm A-okay." Odin's voice was energetic. "Want to stay for dinner?"

"Let's see how it goes. The arm comes first."

"You don't want to miss Crystal's cooking. When she's not down south, the kitchen is her church."

I'd packed a few things in the car and was hoping to get to SunSpot and down to the redwoods before dark. Before that bear began its nocturnal roaming.

At Odin and Crystal's house, an orange Porsche sat where Shannon had parked his truck when we picked up the table. The Odin's Antiques van was nearer the stairs. I parked left of the Porsche, went to the backseat for my doctor's bag. The front door opened. Out came Odin. He lifted his straw hat and danced down the wood stairs. He wasn't wearing a sling. He waved the right arm.

"Wore it until Monday morning. I'm fine. Want to arm wrestle?"

I shook my head. "No handshakes. No pulling on the arm."

Odin gestured to his right, turned in that direction. "We got picnic tables up there. I'll listen to the birds while you take out the stitches."

"With an opening that wide, not for another week. I'll check it and change the bandage. Oh, and watch you put on the sling before I leave."

A gravel trail led to a cement area with two picnic tables running parallel to a shuffleboard court beaming gray under late-afternoon light. The shuffleboard court at Odin and Crystal's house was unique in that rather than having a long triangle at each end, and painted-black zones for points, this one had blue circles with blue peace signs inside them. I didn't inquire about scoring.

Following my eyes, Odin said, "Cool, huh? Crystal's idea."

As if on cue, Crystal Bench emerged from the house. She had a ballerina's combination of an exceptionally slender frame and taut muscles. She smiled as if looking into a camera.

Odin made the introductions.

Crystal gave me a firm handshake. "Welcome to Moonlight Manor."

Probably because she was an actress, and trim in online photographs, I'd imagined Crystal as tall, but she was more sprite than Amazon. She wore a short tangerine-colored dress and brown rope sandals. Silky blonde hair, not quite touching the wiry shoulders, curled forward and up.

Crystal's arms opened wide. "What do you think of our dream land?"

"I can see the work involved. It's great."

Crystal stepped onto the shuffleboard court and fell into a mime routine. Odin tipped his head to a side and rolled his pale eyes in a dismissive manner. Crystal directed traffic at an imaginary four-way stop, employing arm motions and a pretend whistle. This was all done in slow motion, like Tai Chi. She looked behind her as if watching the last car go on its way. Her arms went limp. Her eyes closed, her chin dropped.

One, two, three seconds later Crystal came to life. She smiled brightly. "I'm off to see the wizard."

Crystal skipped her way to the back door.

"I don't get it."

"She's going to start dinner," Odin said.

"What did you tell her about the arm?"

"I cut it on wire sticking out in the store attic. It worked."

Soft blues were present in lengthening shadows. The grounds at Moonlight Manor exuded a nature-as-perfected enchantment. I opened my black bag and, sitting next to Odin at a redwood picnic table, unwrapped the bandage and looked over the wound. It was not coming along as well as Odin thought. The stitches had been strained by exertion. On four the threading wasn't as tight as it should be. The skin there was red and puffy.

Odin said, "Ouch."

"You're going to have more than ouch if you keep pushing it. If you'd worn the sling as instructed, and didn't use your arm, you'd be halfway done now."

"I'm fine," Odin insisted.

I cleaned along the wound, trying to decide whether to start over with a few stitches or let nature take its course. I figured there was no use replacing the loosened stitches; he'd just overdo it again, thinking the replacements could take more strain. Neither of us spoke as I finished with his arm, applied a fresh bandage, left the soiled one on the picnic table and closed the doctor's bag.

Odin said, "I read where your clinic is in a tough spot financially. That it might have to cancel at the end of the year."

"You mean close. We're taking steps to prevent it."

Odin surveyed his dream land. "It'd have to be anonymous, but I'd like to help. I have a thought."

"If you go put on your sling, I'll hear your thought."

Odin shot me a look that said *really*?

"I mean it. You want to talk, put on the sling."

Odin went inside. I looked around at grounds that were borderline manicured, certainly not wild like the surrounding acreage. Plump squirrels romped and made chugging calls louder than the higher-pitched chirps and tweets coming from birds darting tree to tree.

Odin returned, arm in a new-looking sling, and sat across from me. "It's hell driving any distance with my wing like this. But I have obligations. I have an idea. Even though it's short term, it could help a little with your clinic situation."

"Go on."

Odin explained that early Wednesday mornings he made a series of deliveries to restaurants, and a private party, in the East Bay. Door to door the route took approximately six hours. Pay was substantial. If it went to Yates Health, Odin would kick up the proceeds a notch, from five hundred to six hundred dollars.

"What would I be dropping off?"

"Products of value. You wouldn't even have to look at them.

You do the drops until I can drive the van again. You or the clinic pick up an extra six hundred a week. Because I'm sure you work Wednesdays, I'm thinking weekends."

"This clearly isn't legal."

Odin removed his straw hat with his left hand, rubbed it over his light-skinned, bald pate. "Hey. You and I both got bum right wings. You at the bottom, me at the top. Maybe that's a sign."

I stood, grabbed the black bag. "That I'll break the law to help you?"

"To help the clinic, I'll up it to six-fifty a week till I'm back in the saddle. Final offer."

"I haven't heard a word you said, because I've still never been here except the time I bought a table."

Odin caught my eyes with his. "Look, I don't want to lose this gig. He lifted his arm. "The drive hurt like hell today. That's why everything's red. And I gave my word on getting it done."

"My word on this is goodbye."

I walked away. Odin didn't lift his straw hat.

Driving Moonlight Road, shadows becoming darker by the minute, I decided it was too late to head toward the coast to check on Bianca's Teacher Lady. Besides, my time with Odin had generated a sour taste in my mouth, and an overall malaise.

Much of Friday afternoon was taken up by a house call to an elderly woman with diabetes in a boondocks area up north—no town—known as Dorr Place. She lived in what had been her grandparents' house, built of wood milled on the property. Ninety-three years old, Eva Dorr was born there, grew up in those woods and told me she'd never lived anywhere else. She was the kind of patient that made house calls worth any required time and distance. When describing how she felt physically, Eva employed the F-word half a dozen times.

After returning to Yates, I poked my head into Inez's office. "See you tomorrow. I'm taking Bianca to Vertex." This was an indoor rock-climbing facility. "The kids who work there are great with her."

Inherited from the old Yates Grange days, Inez's broad dark wood desk had a PC and keyboard, and two glowing monitors on it. Hunched forward, she blew curly hair away from glasses fronting her intense brown eyes.

"Could you come in for a minute?"

Inez gestured toward the door. I closed it. If Inez's office door was closed, no one entered unless something was urgent.

"Should I come early tomorrow?" I asked.

"Sex is the last thing on my mind right now."

I sat across from her.

Inez said, "If an opportunity comes your way, you might take it."

"Oh?"

"For now, this is between us. I met with the people at Redwood Empire Health. We discussed a possible merger. If Yates has to close, it's the only way our patients won't be stuck with a gap in care."

"They'd have to drive to Santa Rosa. Redwood Empire would never operate out of this building."

"That's a good point. But why stop there?" Inez said. "Why not remind me that for some people up north it'd be a two-hour

39

drive each way? No more mobile care. Many patients wouldn't get their health attended to. Can you think of anything else crappy to remind me of?"

I popped out of the chair, went around the desk and massaged the back of Inez's neck. It was stiff with knots. "I'm sorry."

"It's the truth is what it is."

"I'm still sorry. It was a cheap shot."

Inez reached back with her right arm. She wrapped it around my waist. "Don't go soft on me. I need you to push me until I either come up with something for Yates to survive, or get our people covered by another provider."

"What can I do?"

"Go home. Enjoy the Warriors on TV tonight."

I kissed the top of her head, took in Inez's scent, the reassuring feel of her thick brown hair on my lips.

Inez let go of my waist. "Bianca's having dinner at Ellen's. It'll give me a couple more hours to grind here." Inez took off her glasses, set them between the two lighted screens on her desk. "How about if you kiss me goodbye?"

"I thought you didn't want me to go soft on you."

"I don't. Kiss me as hard as you can."

Seven

Dawn, Sunday, found me at Odin's striking property, climbing into a beige Ford Econoline van with "Simpkins Furniture Delivery and Installation" painted in black across its sides. Stowed behind front seats were sixteen white Styrofoam ice chests, their lids strapped down by bungee cords. They were numbered to match numbers on a sheet of paper Odin had given me. After Friday's conversation with Inez regarding the possible fate of Yates Health, I'd called Odin and told him I'd make the deliveries.

"What's in the ice chests?"

Odin shrugged. "Six hundred and fifty dollars' worth of your time."

"If it's such a secret, why not do it in the middle of the night?"

A smile, suggesting patience. "A delivery truck at two, three in the morning? It would stick out like a broken thumb."

"The saying is 'stick out like a sore thumb.'"

"Whatever. Remember, tear the list into pieces and toss them out the window on the drive back."

"Remember, keep the sling on," I said.

After leaving Moonlight Road for Burnside Road, I drove the

curves for a mile. The Styrofoam boxes squeaked like chalk on a blackboard on the van's metal floor. At a wide spot I parked in the shade of a Douglas fir tree, went to the glove compartment to examine the registration, see who owned the van. The glove box was locked. Having already smelled fish, I reached back and removed a Styrofoam lid. Digging through ice cubes revealed salmon fillets layered between butcher paper; I'd read in the newspaper that salmon season wouldn't start until June. There was also abalone, which everyone knew were under a multi-year harvesting ban. Plus venison and quail. Curiosity soaring, I went to the rear of the van and opened its double doors, discovered two sea turtles among more salmon, abalone, venison, and quail. I re-secured the bungee cords and drove away regretting my probing.

I was doing a wrong thing for a right reason while passing through a slice of heaven on earth. The sky was alive with gigantic swirling white clouds. Between two of them a crescent moon floated in a patch of cobalt blue. After reaching Highway 101, it was south to Marin County, to and over the Richmond-San Rafael Bridge. The first delivery had a Berkeley address. Rather than to behind a restaurant, the route took me way up in the hills to a stone mansion, three stories with a copper roof. It reminded me of a French Chateau. The black iron gate, complete with spikes, was open. The list of drop spots had *next to lamp post* written after the address. The lamp post was at the bottom of stone stairs. One down, seven stops to go. I justified my actions by telling myself that if I weren't making the run, Odin would have paid someone else to do it.

The drops became routine. No looking back and forth when

setting down two Styrofoam ice chests at an assigned spot, be it the bed of a pickup truck, behind a dumpster in an alley behind a restaurant named Les Quatre Saison's, or at a cemetery in the Piedmont hills. I was getting away with something illicit, and enjoyed the feeling. The sheet listing drop spots went into a front pocket of my jeans during the return drive north. I kept it on the off chance I'd somehow get caught.

Odin must have heard tires crunching gravel on Moonlight Road because he was waiting as the beige van climbed the driveway. He gestured toward where I should park. He wore the white sling. It was smudged in a few places. I got out, leaving the keys on the driver's seat as previously instructed. Odin lifted his straw hat, asked if there were any problems.

"None. It was easy."

Odin produced a white envelope. "For your time."

"Money's your department. Send it to Yates Health anonymously."

"Whatever."

"If it shows up at the clinic, this could get done again."

I looked at the redwood house, the grounds, the three-car garage, the orange Porsche. Shannon had been spot-on about the doings of Odin De Laat. No way someone could afford that place by selling what was offered at Odin's Antiques.

"Why hire me, not somebody else?"

Odin's smiles had begun to seem less than sincere. "Because," he said, "you have a lot to lose. Other guys, they might get sloppy. You worried about your career is my insurance policy."

"Go to hell."

"Hell is a possibility. But on the way I'll eat like a king."

Heading for my car, despite conflicting emotions, I felt upbeat. I enjoyed observing how Odin and Crystal had re-shaped the landscape without subjugating it. Everything smelled good out there. All of my life I'd enjoyed being the good kid, later a good citizen, on the outside, and at the same time dodging trouble doing things that were risky. The pattern was baked into me, no matter the consequences.

I drove to SunSpot, and opted not to bring the food I'd packed for Teacher Lady. Encounters with homeless people had taught me that many were insulted by repeated handouts. It was a pride thing, and good because it showed they didn't see themselves as defeated. I ambled down the trail from SunSpot's flat area with buildings. A mile-plus later I reached the brush tunnel and ducked through. Entering the redwood forest was akin to stepping into another world. The distinctive fresh taste of the air. Decades of rotted twigs and brown tree needles under foot. Feeling cleansed of my crimes, I walked to the blue tarp.

"Hello? Are you here?"

As if materializing on the spot, a young woman appeared, not six feet away. Soft-looking brown hair fell in a stream to the middle of her back. It was kept in place by a curved wooden hair clip. Her eyes were of no discernible color. Maybe five feet five, light skinned, a chin that curved to a point. White legs beneath a very old fashioned looking dress that touched her shins, printed in overlapping green squares. Bare feet. Her gaze released a calming warmth. Her voice conveyed the same.

"I presume you are Doctor Taylor. If not, please leave me be."

She set her feet, getting ready to run.

"Yes, Jeff Taylor. I'm hoping you'll talk with me."

"If you tell anyone about my visitation, I won't be able to do what I've been sent here for. It happened once. I disappeared."

"What were you sent here for?"

"I never know until it happens."

"Until what happens?"

"I don't know." Other than her mouth, she didn't move when speaking. "What I know is, I wake up somewhere and wait for it to transpire."

Playing along with her, I said, "How long does it take?"

She sat without a sound. A hand gently pushed the hem of her dress down between her knees. "Usually not this prolonged. I've had to establish a life. I never had to do that the other times."

I sat across from Teacher Lady. "I don't understand."

She grinned. "I found a way to generate income, from something I used to do. It shall sustain me while I await what I'm here for."

Teacher Lady's calm vitality soothed me. Rare for me, I felt wholly relaxed and not afraid to speak my mind.

"I'm trying to help a health clinic where I work. We can't keep up with the bills. I've started bringing in extra income, but it's illegal." The words burbled forth. It was as if someone else were speaking. "What do you think? Should I keep doing it?"

"Do your good where it does the most. That's what Mr. Burbank used to say."

"Are you talking about Luther Burbank, the plant person?"

Teacher Lady giggled airily. It reminded me of someone; I couldn't think of who. "Do your good where it does the most. I think of that, waiting for what I was sent here for."

"Can I ask you about something?"

"Yes."

"The bear that scared the hell out of me? I worried about it, coming here. How come you weren't scared?"

Another giggle reminding me of that person I couldn't bring to mind. "We don't need to talk about it. The bear went away."

"How do you know?"

"There are no females in the vicinity. It went in search of a mate."

"What makes you so sure?"

Teacher Lady smiled easily, stood. She did not swat away twigs and needles; none clung to her dress or legs. "I think this is where people, in these times, recite 'have a nice day.'"

I got up from the bed of redwood duff, bent over and flicked bits of it off my jeans, and plucked redwood needles that had lodged between shoelaces. I looked up to say goodbye. Teacher Lady was gone.

Eight

Midweek, Inez the sent staff a peppy email. The morning's mail had contained an envelope with thirteen fifty-dollar bills inside it, sent anonymously to Yates Health. *This is a small but emblematic show of support. West County folks care! Since the newspaper article, we're getting donations every day. You're making a difference in people's lives.*

I called Odin and said I'd examine his stitches on Sunday, after returning from a second round of illegal food drops, thereby earning another six hundred and fifty dollars for the clinic. I'd match that, anonymously. In a couple of weeks salary cuts for Inez, Sandy, Suzanne and I would kick in. My aim was to help keep the clinic limping along until Inez scored a grant or a sponsorship, or both.

Sunday's drop list was the same as before. After leaving two Styrofoam ice chests at the stone mansion in the Berkeley hills, I descended to flatlands. Drop number two was at an alley behind a mini strip mall in a dicey neighborhood near the Berkeley-Oakland border.

Put behind door--knock leave.

The alley was narrow. You had to go slow around dumpsters.

Glancing in the rear-view mirror brought a chill down my spine and instant heat to my cheeks; a gray pickup truck entered the lane. Odin had said if I saw anyone near a drop, keep going. Text him the number of the skipped site, remain on course and return to it after the other drops were completed. Odin would text the recipient an explanation for the booty not coming within its assigned thirty-minute slot. Not a problem.

Not a problem until a low-slung old Chevy Impala, its front fenders swathed in grayish body filler, entered the other end of the alley. I put my arm out and motioned for the Chevy's driver—a man—to back up. He did not. He didn't stop advancing until he was twenty feet in front of me. I looked to read the front license plate. There wasn't one. The driver hopped out. Likely in his thirties, he wore a purple surgical mask and a dark baseball cap pulled low. He stood in front of the Impala and pointed a pistol at me.

"Get out. Look down. Don't look at me. C'mon, now!"

Climbing out, my gaze stayed downward.

"Nose on the ground," the man ordered. "Hands wrapped behind your head. Lift your nose, I'll blow it off."

The handles of the van's rear doors made noises of being opened.

"It's all yours. I'm just delivery."

"Shut up."

Behind me came squeaks as Styrofoam ice chests were dragged across the floor of the van. I worried someone might come along, see the scene and there'd be trouble. That maybe the gun would be fired. What had I gotten myself into? An easy money lark of a task had changed, within seconds, into something entirely different. I heard the driver of the pickup climb all the way into the van.

His voice was low, steady, that of a man much older than the one pointing the gun. "Keep your head down after we leave. My partner, over there? He's crazy. Try to follow us, you could end up dead. Understand?"

"Yes."

The man made more trips to his pickup and back. The engines of two vehicles came alive. There wasn't room enough to drive past the van. Both vehicles had to exit the short passageway in reverse. Reeling through my head was the image of an outstretched arm with a hand holding a pistol aimed at me. I looked up, looked around. The truck and Chevy Impala were gone. I got in the van, left the alley and parked on a side street. That's when the shaking began. In no condition to drive, I locked the van and walked the neighborhood, walked until my steps felt normal, then went to a corner market for peanut butter cookies and water. Back in the van, the drop list was folded and slipped it into a front jeans pocket.

I texted Odin: *Only one completed.*

Near the end of the return drive, on Burnside Road, an orange Porsche whizzed past going the opposite direction. Crystal gaped at seeing the van. She was traveling at an unsafe speed.

Odin came outside and descended the stairs as the van climbed the driveway. A dish towel showing red was wrapped around his upper right arm. So he'd finally overdone it. I took satisfaction in that, set the van's key on the driver's seat, and got out.

Wide-eyed, bald head bright under midday sun, Odin said, "What the hell happened?"

We both stopped walking.

I pointed to his arm and the bloody dish towel. "What the hell happened?"

Pale eyes blazed. "An unfortunate misunderstanding."

"With whoever shot you during the other misunderstanding?"

"Hey. I need doctoring."

"Crystal just passed me on Burnside. Fast. Is everything okay?"

Odin treated me to one of his reflexive smiles. "She went for a Sunday drive. When she's not trapped in L.A., she likes to get out and about."

"You're a bullshit machine. She was driving like a maniac. I'll get my medical bag."

"I want to know what happened down there," Odin said.

"Because you're so concerned about me, right?"

Odin's voice rose to match mine. "My concern is product wasn't delivered. You haven't told me the extent of loss. I'll be inside. I've got to sit down."

I turned and headed for the Subaru.

A bath towel was opened on the dining table. Two clean dish towels were stacked next to it. Odin went to take off a blood-stained, short-sleeved shirt, grunted and gave up. I snipped off the sleeve. Odin's stitches were gone. It wasn't a pretty sight. He was in pain and experiencing pain often aids in people wanting to talk. I gave him shots of Lidocaine directly above and directly below the wound. Odin watched the needle pierce his skin.

He said, "What happened?"

"You mean, what happened to your, quote, product? Two guys sandwiched me with their vehicles in the alley at number two. One pointed a gun at me. Made me get on the ground, face down. They took it all."

Odin looked to the table, thinking. Or maybe doing math. "No warning?"

"Any hint of a hassle, I would've skipped the drop."

Good god, I thought. Now I'm even talking like a criminal. I worked on the mess where the stitches had been. "I'm shaken because a guy threatened to kill me if I didn't do precisely what he said. What's your excuse?"

"My visitors got calls from three customers who didn't get their deliveries. Numbers two, four and five. Number two didn't find anything at the door even an hour after the scheduled time. He finally calls the supplier. The supplier's associates came by to wait for me to get back. Obviously, I was already here. Then Crystal returns from the farmer's market. She sees my arm, hops in the car and takes off."

No comment from me. I examined Odin's original slice, deciding how to approach suturing the reopened wound. "You lost me on the wait for you to get back part."

"They didn't know about the arm grazing. They'd been trying to scare me that time, about another matter. They didn't know I wasn't driving the route. I'd told them we should switch to Sundays because it seemed safer. Less traffic. When they found me here, they went ballistic. They made a call."

"A call to who?"

Odin shook his head. "Just fix the arm."

"Not until you tell me more about your visitors."

I went to the kitchen, took a glass from a cupboard, filled the glass with water and drank it leaning against the tile counter. Odin's bare arm, with the dish towel removed, bled markedly.

"You could go to the emergency room in Appleton," I said. "You could explain to them what happened with your arm."

"Okay. You'll find out eventually. My visitors—"

"How many?"

Most people in his condition would be whimpering. Odin was simply tense.

"Two. They wanted to know why I hid not doing the driving. I showed them my arm. They wanted to know who drove instead."

"Shit."

The more upset Odin became, the more extreme his Scandinavian accent became. "I wouldn't tell 'em. I said the driver wouldn't steal. Doesn't need to."

"They obviously didn't go for it."

"Pinned me on the floor, right by where you are. Put cuffs on me. One goes to the car for pliers. He ripped the stitches out, one at a time, until I coughed up your name. Then he ripped out the last ones, I guess to make a point."

"I've heard enough. Now shut up, or I'll leave you as you are."

I needed to think things through.

After restitching the wound, I didn't close the door on the way out. On Moonlight Road, gravel under the tires sounded extra loud. The road ahead appeared to bounce up and down.

Odin had surrendered my name to a man who ripped out his stitches with a pair of pliers. I was returning to a converted garage set at the back end of a deep lot. I never entertained visitors. Now it seemed only a matter of time before some came knocking.

Nine

Sitting mid-block on Main Street, Yates General was in a 1940s wood structure made all the quainter because it needed a fresh coat of paint. A relaxed, everybody's welcome atmosphere permeated the store. A large yellow sun, its beams widening toward their ends, was painted on a wall above wood bins laden with fruits and vegetables. Lots of long hair on both genders. Yates General was perhaps two-thirds groceries and one-third a gallery of pottery, paintings, books, and items like handmade greeting cards, all created by locals.

Turning over a turquoise-glazed bowl in my hands, I saw two colored pencil botanical drawings, maybe twelve inches high and ten inches across, propped up on a white shelf above ceramic bowls. Prices were listed; the artist was not named. They looked, in their exactitude, like the one in Teacher Lady's abode. I went to a desk situated between the artsy stuff and the food aisles.

A man stood. "May I help you?"

In his sixties, hair silvery yet full, the man gave off a laid-back vibe. Reading glasses hung from a black band and rested on his chest. He wore an untucked off-white shirt. His face and eyes showed he'd spent much of his life outdoors.

"Can you look at something with me?" I asked.

"Of course." When I stopped in front of the pottery and drawings, he put out his hand. "Kurt Sanderson."

"Jeff Taylor."

We shook. He glanced at my disfigured hand. "You're the new doctor." Sanderson set the bowl I'd looked at back in its proper spot. He ran a finger along its rim. "John Chambers. He's the real thing."

"Actually, I'm interested in those two drawings. There's no name on them."

Sanderson nodded, slowly, genially.

"I've met the person who did them. She's friendly, but mysterious. I'm curious to know more about her."

Sanderson put on his glasses and examined the drawings. "There's something special about these. It's hard to describe. It's like they're more real than real."

"What's her name?"

Sanderson stepped back, let the glasses fall. "Don't know. She comes in, gives me a drawing. I give her a note to take to the cash register when she buys food. She's bought blankets, too. I don't know what else. Oh, when she comes in, she puts on a pair of tennis shoes from the freebie bin, because I told her health department rules say no shoes, no service. On her way out, she drops the shoes back in the bin."

"Does she strike you as, you know, slightly off?"

Sanderson seemed amused. "Doctors always want to find something wrong with people."

"I'm worried she's mentally unbalanced in a way that might be harmful to her."

"One thing you should know about West County," Sanderson said, "is we respect each other's privacy."

"Fair enough. I'll take them both."

Sanderson resumed the slow nodding. "How about if you choose one? Two would make me worry you might be getting creepy about her."

I held my tongue.

"The one of grass and white butterflies."

Sanderson reached over the pottery and took the drawing off the shelf.

"Do other people want to know the artist's name?" I asked.

"Other people like the mystery. And don't ask a lot of questions." Sanderson handed me the drawing. "They'll ring this up for you in front."

To the right upon entering my rental were a small bathroom with a shower, and a petite bedroom that allowed for a single mattress set on a wood pallet. The rest of the place was a garage's rectangle with a large square window at the far end. The window faced a sloping acre of untended apple trees. Beyond them stood a nicely kept up, watery green two-story house. Often on weekends smoke from a steel barbecue, visible on the back deck, wafted across the apple orchard. Sounds of good cheer would remind me that I lived alone in a little house without halls.

It had been a taxing day. I fell into a twitchy, dreams-filled sleep on the living room couch. In one dream Teacher Lady emerged from behind one redwood tree after another, spilling airy giggles. Knocking at the front and only door roused me. I remembered Odin's arm and that his stitches had been ripped out. Getting up, shaking myself awake, I went to the kitchen.

Through the door came, "I know you're home. You car's here."

I grabbed a butcher's knife and went to the door. "Who is it?"

"Duh. It's Shannon."

"Are you alone?"

"Seriously. We got to talk."

At opening the door, I looked past Shannon and around the area where my car and Shannon's faded blue truck were parked. To the right the yard went downhill, with plenty of trees to hide behind. Left was a concrete retaining wall that had an opening behind its end, where the garbage and recycling containers were stored. It would be easy for Odin's tormentors to find out where I lived.

Shannon's eyes widened at seeing the knife. He smelled strongly of beer. "I seen your name somewhere."

Shannon motioned to the knife, then lowered his hand in suggestion. He looked like something bad had happened. I waved him in, shut the door. I set the knife on the coffee table, sat on the couch and gestured toward the only armchair in the house, a plum-colored one I'd found on a sidewalk with a 'FREE' sign on it.

Shannon paced back and forth behind the chair. The teak table we'd put in the back of his truck was in plain view. It didn't garner a remark.

"What is it?" I asked.

His eyes gleamed like Christmas lights. "I don't know if I should tell you. But I guess it's too late." Shannon ceased pacing. "Do you have any beer?"

"Not for you. Sit down. You make me nervous."

Shannon sat. Lifting his short brown ponytail with one hand, he rubbed beneath it with the other. His eyes were more red than white. "I do painting for someone north of the river, on Ridge Road. You know it?"

"I've been on it for house calls."

"Every month or so he wants a new color for this big room where he holds meetings, these things he calls The Sessions. It's like he gets a whim, it has to be done fast. Which is cool. He pays great."

Shannon's breath would have earned him an invitation to step out of the vehicle at any DUI checkpoint.

"His paying well can't be why you're here."

Shannon grabbed both flabby red cheeks and tugged outwards. "I'm in his study, on a step ladder filling in where wall meets ceiling. I step down and look over at a desk. There's this notepad with your name in big letters across the top. Nothin' else."

"He's probably going to schedule an appointment."

"He's got medical people come to *him*. He's rich."

"Okay. Why are you worried he wrote down my name?"

"Because his hands are in a lot of dirty stuff. If he has a problem with somebody, they tend to end up hurt. That's the word, anyway."

For the second time on that long, miserable Sunday, an icy chill ran down my spine.

Shannon pushed on his knees, got to his feet. He blew out hard, scratched his bulbous head violently. "I got to slow down. You sure you don't have a beer? One beer?"

"I'm sure. What's the man's name?"

For the first time since I'd known him, Shannon was not quick on the talk trigger. He looked down. He spoke softly. "Alex Moran. You didn't hear it from me. Maybe it's a mistake to tell you, but I thought you should know he has your name."

"Okay. Thanks."

I'd never heard of Alex Moran. Shannon's fear in speaking his name sent alarm bells ringing. Shannon was the kind of man you'd want on your side in a street brawl.

"I should go," Shannon said. "Maybe I should've kept my mouth shut."

He left with his chin down. The last thing he said was, "Be careful. You don't know what you're dealing with."

I lasted an hour before finally giving in and contacting Inez. We shared a code phrase when either of us wanted to meet for sex. I texted, *olive oil.*

Will try came in a minute.

Linda Wilson, mother of Bianca's best friend Ellen, was seeing a carpenter in Graton named Jay. Linda and Inez had what they termed a single-mom pact wherein, if possible, one covered for the other when a tryst was on the horizon. This included school nights. Inez had Bianca packed and delivered to Ellen's in thirty minutes. I had a house key and waited in bed for Inez's return. The moment she entered the bedroom she began undressing.

"Whatever you had for lunch," Inez said, "make it a habit."

"Noted."

We started slow. We didn't stay slow. We plowed into each other. I drove into Inez's center as fast and deeply as I could, flipping my body inside-out, over and over, as pleasure soared.

A panel in the bed frame split. Inez convulsed. White lights exploded in my head.

Everything stopped. For how long, I cannot say. Closing my eyes, dizzy, I pressed Inez against me.

"You're desperate." Inez's words were slurred. "I can tell. What's wrong?"

"Fear of death."

"Are you joking?"

"No."

"Okay. Why do you fear death today?"

"I do every day. Some days it's just more acute."

Next to each other, gazing upwards, Inez patted my thigh, then left her hand on it.

"I like it when you're a little weird," she said.

"Do you know that after a man is hung, when they take him down there's always semen in his underwear? It's like a last spurt of life. Fear of death fuels the survival instinct."

Inez removed her hand from my leg. "I know we said no rules. But I think we should have one."

The surfaces of every object in the room were extraordinarily vivid.

"Like?"

"No talking right after sex. We should stay with it longer. As long as we can."

"Not a problem."

Inez said, "You want a rule?"

"One's enough."

Inez turned onto her side. I matched her; we were face to face. She ran a hand over my thinning, damp brown hair. "Did anyone ever tell you, under your easy-going surface, you're the most intense person they've ever met?"

"Yeah."

"And?"

"So far, being like I am hasn't worked out with anyone over the long haul. Karen stuck with me five years. No one else for long at all. Other than you and Karen, no other relationship of any significance. It always comes back to something inside me that wants to fail. I seem to have a need to screw things up."

"Want to talk about it?"

"Not now," I said.

"When?"

"When I understand it better."

Ten

Having left the backpack with non-perishable food, a set of colored pencils and stiff drawing paper in my car's trunk for days, after work on Tuesday, I headed for SunSpot Preserve. Duncan's Valley Road climbed through redwoods. It leveled off. The land opened to both sides. A few turns and I entered Duncan's Valley itself. A black Ford Explorer showed in my rear-view mirror. Speeding toward me, its image swelled. At a straightway it roared, swinging into the middle of the road.

The Explorer passed and veered toward me, forcing me to skid into the parking area of an abandoned farmhouse with plywood-covered windows. My car stopped facing a grassy upslope with redwood trees atop its crest. The large car blocked any possible exit. A shiny black Cadillac Escalade, worthy of a presidential motorcade, rolled up behind the Explorer. Trapped again.

A tall, burly fellow climbed down from the Explorer. He had a long, dark beard and looked to be in his thirties. He approached in steps where, wide as he was, the front leg went a bit sideways and back to center as he advanced. Solace was taken in that he wasn't brandishing a pistol. I lowered the window.

The man approached with hands dangling at his sides. He spoke politely. "Mr. Moran will share social discourse with you now."

The driver's door of the black Escalade popped open. A replica of the Explorer's heavy driver, including the dark beard, appeared and walked around the nose of the muscular vehicle. He opened a rear door. Out stepped a man I estimated to be in his early fifties, with cropped short hair dyed a sparkling champagne blond. He nodded to his driver, shot the cuffs of a long-sleeved black turtleneck shirt and walked toward me. I climbed out and looked across the rising field with redwood trees at the top, pretending not to be scared. The blond man, on the short side yet sturdy, approached. I offered my bad hand.

"Dr. Taylor," he said. "I am Mr. Moran."

He did not shake hands.

"Call me Jeff."

"I call you what I choose." His words were delivered in a kind of straight line. No rise and fall in tone. "You-are-to-call-me-Mr.-Moran."

I leaned against my car door. The identical tough guys stood with legs apart, hands behind their backs. One positioned himself adjacent to his boss. The other stayed in front of my car, perhaps anticipating I might take off running up the hill. Their long dark beards were trimmed exactly alike. They were rectangles.

"You and I have a problem," Moran said. "A four thousand nine hundred dollar problem. Seven times seven hundred."

"How can we? We've never met."

Moran looked at me disapprovingly. He slowly shook his

small head, which for an unknown reason reminded me of a child's globe. "You are not allowed to waste my minutes pretending not to know."

Marbly green eyes seemed to see through me into another dimension. His cheeks and forehead were covered with a faint dusting of face powder.

"I'm not the reason your minutes are ticking by," I said. "Your people stopped me."

Moran stepped in close. He smelled like peaches. "I've been to see the Dutchman, who hid that his right arm is not up to the required driving. His fault, for engaging in a falsehood. He explained you took my cargo for a fee. We went to Yates and waited for you to exit your workday. You-are-to-tell-me-everything."

I explained Yates Health's need for infusions of cash, and described making the first run without incident. Next I described the holdup, in detail, so there was no doubting its violent threat.

"When I got to Odin's," I said, "the stitches in his right arm had been ripped out. Ripping them out caused the man to lose significant blood. Are these two the—"

Moran's hands flew out wide, palms forward. Both goons reached to the rear waist bands of their jeans.

"Not that," Moran said, keeping his penetrating, swami-like gaze locked on me. "I am informing Dr. Taylor he has wandered off topic."

In chorus, like marines, the thugs said, "Yes, sir."

Moran's tongue darted out and back in, like a snake's. "Cargo has been going south for a significant amount of time. Odin says this was only your second trip. How did the perpetrators know about Sunday? Did you tip them off?"

"No. The only thing I could think of is a customer at the restaurant has eaten your… cargo. It comes in illegally. It wouldn't be hard to stake out the place, see when and how it arrives."

Moran seemed an eccentric mixture of a New Age guru and an articulate, if undersized, crime boss. "Interesting theory. Did either of the thieves look like they have means to dine on that caliber of fare?"

"I didn't see the older one. He sounded—I can't say. I was going to say he sounded educated, but I don't really know."

"I know what I paid for the cargo. Since it wasn't delivered, money has to be credited to my clients, but one. You were last to possess. You are to work something out with Odin. A heads up. De Laat is broke. That's why he attached himself to me in the first place."

"I think this is between you and Odin, not Odin and—"

"Done!" Moran walked away, trailing the peaches smell. He did not look back. The goons hurried their wide bodies to vehicles. "Balance is four-nine. Via De Laat."

The big dark machines, spreading dust, turned around and rolled back toward Yates. I was too full of pumping adrenaline to get in the car right away.

I hit Odin's number. No answer. I left a message.

"They came looking for me. I hope Moran had 'em rip out the new stitches." I forced myself to hold back. I had not been coerced into making the deliveries. "Whatever goes on between you and those people is none of my business. Keep me out of it."

I clicked off. Walking circles on the gravel, I left another message.

"If those guys come after me again, I won't hesitate to contact the police. Level with them about trying to raise funds for the clinic. I know damn well you have more to hide than delivering illegal food, which itself is not small-time. Fix it so I don't have to go to the police. I don't have a record. I wouldn't go to jail. What about you?"

I hung up and continued driving through Duncan's Valley. The brown Subaru climbed to the ridge with a view of the ocean, and along Tomales Bay to the hills beyond. I parked and walked downhill from SunSpot's flat area. I didn't note the beauty of land not changed by human endeavors, or receive nature's abundant scents. My mind replayed the encounter with strange Alex Moran until I entered the redwoods. It was much cooler than when coming down the open space of the hill. Teacher Lady stepped out from between two trees. Her greenish dress was thin, short sleeved. Her feet were bare.

We exchanged hellos.

"I was wondering, don't you get cold, living out here?"

Teacher Lady only smiled.

"You really never get cold?"

"When I was a child I did. Not anymore."

"Do you ever get scared, being out here alone?"

Teacher lady shook her head. She walked to the blue tarp and unhooked it. "You are my guest. Please sit on the blankets."

I ducked, entered on hands and knees, sat on the tan blankets. Teacher Lady settled onto the mulch. I slipped off the day pack filled with food and drawing materials, and set what I'd brought between us.

"Thank you, Dr. Taylor."

Teacher Lady found slots for the food and drawing materials. The items seemed to disappear into the borders of the teepee-like shelter.

"Call me Jeff."

She sat and pressed her dress down with a hand. Her face was lighter than the low light coming through the opening.

"You can refer to me as Edwina, or Miss Seeba, whichever you think is more appropriate."

"Let's go with Edwina."

Warmth, ease, and a leisurely feeling of security filled the tent-like space. My fears of the previous hour melted away. I heard myself telling Edwina about the dream of her popping out from behind redwood trees. "You were happy."

Edwina giggled. It struck me who her giggles reminded me of. I'd watched a documentary about the Dalai Lama. Same giggle. Same lightness to it.

"I'm not being a good hostess," Edwina said. "Shall we partake in the figs?"

Sharing her one plate, we ate the dried figs I'd brought.

"Where do you come from?" I asked.

"From here."

"From inside this tree?"

A light titter. "From West County."

"And you knew Luther Burbank?"

"As well as anyone at his Appleton farm did."

"I bought one of your drawings at Yates General. The one

with white butterflies. Where did you learn to draw like that?"

"At Mr. Burbank's farm. In high school, I went there after classes and worked in the gardens. Or pulled weeds. Instead of paying me, Mr. Burbank purchased pencils and paper. During summer, or any time it was hot, he let me stay inside the cottage and draw. I'd draw all day."

Did Edwina know about Luther Burbank from books? Was it right to leave her be out there?

Sounds came from outside. They stopped. Fear rose through me like a hot, sour liquid. In one second I jumped from peacefulness to fight or flight mode.

"Did you hear that?" I asked.

"Yes. It's a mother and her fawn. Your voice probably confuses them."

"How do you know it's deer?"

"We see each other. They pass through the fence to better eating places than these woods, which are good for hiding."

Seated on the tan blankets, worried about what might happen with Moran, I felt dumber than ever for getting involved with Odin and that mess. Edwina plainly felt no need to chat. Neither did I. It was nice to be still, to not ask questions, to not try to figure out the nature of this creature sitting close to me. When it began to grow dark, and we could scarcely see each other, Edwina backed out of the tree trunk hut.

"I'll walk you to the fence," she said.

At reaching the brush tunnel, we said goodbyes. Crawling through, I heard Edwina's disembodied voice. "Everything is okay."

Eleven

I often drove past the sign for Luther Burbank's Experiment Farm, near downtown Appleton, but had never thought to stop in. Its paths led you around a few acres. Along the way, low signs gave the names of a particular plant, bush or tree. The farm had a royal hybrid black walnut from the late 1800s, fruit trees, mulch piles, potted plants for sale on the honor system, and a small cottage painted yellow. After walking the grounds, I crossed onto the next parcel, a weedy cemetery, and searched the rows of gravestones for any with the name Seeba carved into it. No luck.

That search, however, led to thinking I might be able to find an obituary for an Edwina Seeba online.

Later, at home. I found no standard obituary, but clicking around the internet I came upon archives of the *Santa Rosa Daily Democrat*. An Edwina Seeba was in an article dated October 24, 1922.

ANOTHER AUTOMOBILE VICTIM

Miss Edwina Seeba, a young woman, met death yesterday, another victim of the proliferation of automobiles in daily life. Miss Seeba grew to womanhood in Appleton and lived there the duration of her years.

The tragedy occurred at the corner of Walters and Adzer streets in the Business District of Appleton. Clayton Cook, driver of the car, always considered a careful man, initiated a right turn onto Adzer Street. There is no sign signaling a stop. Mr. Cook did not see Miss Seeba crossing the street. Two wheels passed over her body. Sheriff Jedediah Fry stated it was an unfortunate accident.

Miss Seeba is survived by her mother, Mrs. Constance Seeba. Her father, Mr. Timothy Seeba, succumbed to the Spanish flu in 1919. Miss Seeba's brother, Armin, four years senior, also succumbed to the Spanish flu in 1919. Much sympathy is expressed for Mrs. Seeba in the sad bereavement that has overtaken her.

Body tingling, I got up from the couch. Thoughts raced in a mixture of wonder, anxiety and confusion. No way could I share this with anyone. It would only open a Pandora's box of unknowns with the exception that I'd be known as loony. After calming down, I searched for more information and couldn't find any. No funeral announcement. No mention of the so-called careful Mr. Cook being cited for killing somebody with his car.

Had Edwina read the account and imagined herself as the young woman run over by a car in 1922? That seemed impossible, yet it was the most likely explanation for her strange words.

Odin didn't answer calls or texts. I couldn't decide if it would be better to drive to Moonlight Road and confront him, or let him worry about what action I might take. I opted to stay away until something new developed.

During days, emotions were heightened. Changes I was going through made me both more alive to the nuances of the present, and feeling removed from what was going on in the larger world.

A week passed without a further incident involving Odin or Moran. Saturday morning, after dropping Bianca and Ellen at the high school for open gym, Inez came home to me waiting in her bed. Without saying hello, Inez looked right at me as she undressed and slid under the blankets.

"Are you seeing someone?" Inez drew her face away. "You're different. I feel it every time we talk. No scenes if you are."

Though I wasn't cheating on Inez, I didn't want to even approach the subject. I kissed her cheek.

"I asked you a question," Inez said.

"Of course I'm not seeing anybody else. I've got a lot going on in my head. If you think it's affecting my work, tell me. Other than that, I need some space right now."

"I don't know what to do. You're lovable, as in crazy lovable. You're also a distant son of a bitch sometimes."

Inez rubbed her chin into my chest, then into the collar bone. The act contained a hint of aggression, yet no anger. Her skin was pleasantly warm against mine.

"I'm damaged goods," I said. "I'm not consistent."

"The other time you said that, I thought it was an excuse for not getting closer. I guess I mean for not committing. Which is stronger? You don't want to let anyone in all the way, or you're trying to protect me from eventually getting hurt?"

"They're both pretty strong."

Inez lifted her head, looked at me. "I've taken refuge in telling myself you're complicated."

"I wouldn't make that claim."

"What do you want to do? Now, in bed."

"Hold you."

"You have two hours. Wake me up half an hour before Bianca comes home."

That afternoon I took Bianca to Vertex for another climbing lesson. Back in Appleton, I just dropped her off because there was the once-a-month Saturday neighborhood potluck I always avoided. On the way home, my phone jingled. I didn't recognize the number.

"Hello."

"Mr. Moran."

On the phone his voice sounded computer generated. I pulled over, and tried to talk in a way that confused him.

"It's really nice to hear from you. Thanks for calling. How's it going?"

"Um, okay." It took a few seconds for Moran to get on course. "There is no reason we can't settle this. I'm granting you an opportunity to atone. Be-at-Odin's at five-sharp."

Odin was more the object of the man's wrath than I. And avoiding his goons forever was not possible.

"Sounds great. I look forward to it."

The black Ford Expedition was a bulky presence dead center in the parking area. To its right, the white Odin's Antiques van. No orange Porsche. I pulled around to the left. The heart started up its faster beating. Odin came down the path from the park-like garden. He wasn't wearing a sling.

Odin lifted his straw hat. "We're up top."

I followed him to the picnic tables adjacent to the shuffleboard court with blue peace signs at each end. Everywhere I looked were blooming flowers and trimmed green bushes. White roses as big as dinner plates. Birds and squirrels cavorted. It was an Edenic setting maintained by crooked acts.

We sat. Across from us sat Moran in a long-sleeved black turtleneck. The helmet cut, champagne-colored hair atop his undersized head made him appear impish. A little face powder, and the peaches smell. His green eyes trained themselves on me.

"Where are your buddies?" I asked.

Moran's tongue appeared and withdrew in about a tenth of a second. "I didn't think Odin would feel comfortable in their presence. We're congregating here today as friends."

"Happy to hear it," I said.

Odin glanced over at me like I was nuts.

Moran's eyes stayed trained on mine. "How long before he can drive the route?"

"At least two more weeks, because of what happened to the first set of stitches."

No change in expression from Moran. He said, "You can't drive on Wednesdays. You drive tomorrow, you drive the next Sunday, I'll call it even. The restaurant where you had an altercation has been eliminated from the route." Moran's head swiveled. His swami eyes pounced on Odin. "You're off two Sundays. You begin driving again on Wednesdays, a week after that." Then to me: "Odin explained how you only took the assignment in order to raise money for the clinic. I admit I did not believe your story. After each of your runs, I'll send a check for seven hundred and fifty to Yates Health. It will solidify my reputation as a community leader."

Playing to the man's vanity, I said, "A thousand would completely cement your reputation as a West County leader."

"You're on."

"That's generous."

"It is not. The money will come from Odin's earnings. He gets nothing until he atones for misleading me. Goodbye. Odin and I have additional business to discuss."

Odin's fair skin burned red. He stared at me like he wanted to do me harm.

I smiled. The smile probably looked as fake as it was. I stood, clapped Odin on his left shoulder. "Have a nice day." I started down the gravel path.

Moran called after me. "One more thing."

I stopped walking. "What's that?"

"You still have one good hand. No need to risk it."

"Have a nice day."

I continued down the path, got in my car and drove away. On the fly I'd considered various aspects of the situation, their possible outcomes, and concluded that venturing out early two Sunday mornings was safer than receiving visits from large men who carried firearms in the back waist bands of their pants.

Twelve

My stomach churned on Sunday's dawn drive to Moonlight Road. Waiting in the parking area at Odin's, its nose pointed forward, was the beige Ford van with "Simpkins Furniture Moving and Installation" painted along its sides. A key rested on the delivery list, which was on the passenger's seat. Odin did not come outside. I adjusted the seat to fit my long legs and headed out in the day's first light.

When making drop number one at the Berkeley hills mansion, my anxiety level stayed low. Once I got to the flatlands and had to use alleys and rear parking lots—and a cemetery—every delivery left me with sweaty palms. Why was I doing this? Inez. She represented beliefs I shared yet didn't pursue with anything close to her dogged commitment. If I could help keep the clinic sputtering along for a few more months, I had no doubt that Inez would put together funding necessary to sustain her vision of helping others. Frightened the whole time, the route seemed to take much longer than that first clean run, even with one less delivery.

I dropped off the van. That Odin did not appear was fine by me. At home I felt restless. Couldn't focus on reading or watching a movie on my laptop. I went for a half-hour run at the high school and did some push-ups, which helped. For a while. Doing dishes, I stared across the apple orchard, wondering what it was like to have friends and family over for barbecues. A realization washed over me like a cold ocean wave, a sleeper wave one isn't prepared for. It towed me under, emotionally speaking. I'd grown up in a converted barn and there I was, pushing forty years old, living in a converted garage. Until high school I'd spent an inordinate amount of time alone, wandering in a redwood forest. Now I spent an inordinate amount of time alone, looking out a window at an apple orchard no one was taking care of. I told myself that my work made up for whatever else my life lacked and immediately knew that was a lie.

At six-thirty I headed out on foot, angling across town to Homer's Café. Traffic was brisk on two-lane Highway 116. Homer's Café was a familiar place with familiar sounds and familiar smells. Waitress Kendra smiled in a way that caused me to flatter myself.

Part way through a leisurely meal, the food shimmered. The chicken quesadilla tasted normal, as did a bottle of Sierra Nevada Pale Ale. I knew for sure something was wrong when everything in front of me threw off orange and amber light. I looked around at a world askew. All of the angles were wrong. People's voices were muffled, like they came through dense curtains. The voices echoed and seemed to contain a physical quality. I put a twenty-dollar bill on the table, left without saying goodbye to Kendra, and headed for home.

Holding onto the crosswalk sign pole, I watched the green *WALK* light on the other side of the street count down seconds.

The numbers jumped around and were an astonishing, phosphorescent green that reminded me of creatures seen on an ocean floor. I watched the seconds tick down with fascination, then remembered to cross. Headlights whirled. A horn honked.

The Safeway store, with its high curving roof, looked like a circus tent. I laughed and passed its phantasmagoria of lights that blinked the same orange and amber of inside Homer's Cafe. I wondered what drugs had been slipped into the water glass when I'd gone to the restroom. That must have been what happened. It would not have been Kendra's doing. Maybe twenty people were in the café. I wasn't able to picture them.

Which regulars had been there? I couldn't think straight, couldn't remember.

Stopping at a corner, a streetlight illuminated my hands. Turning them over, observing the changing orange-amber of my palms, I watched a miracle: the pores of my hands breathed. I brought them to my eyes. Each pore opened and closed like slow heartbeats. My fingertips were light sticks. It seemed I'd known this, eons before, and was only now remembering it.

Angling across Forester Park was a shortcut to home. My feet left pavement and started across grass. A loud *whoosh*: the park's sprinklers kicked on in concert-like unison. Water sprayed in colorful orange-amber arcs, soaking me. I marveled at it. Its cool taste was wonderful.

Beyond the area being watered was a baseball field. Heads covered in black veils, their cloaks snowy white, black rosary beads in hands, two nuns shuffled along between the bases. In the middle of the baseball infield, white lilies sprang from the grass, one after another, fully my height. I understood. The nuns were praying for my salvation. I'd been guided to that site, at that hour, to die.

I looked to my hands. Their pores no longer breathed. The palms were merely wet.

To avoid the praying nuns, I went to push my way through the calla lily forest. No resistance. I passed right through them. The lilies were sheer images. Everything began to blink, slowly, blackness, then the askew world of amber, orange and now blue. The colors turned faint. A signal that my time was up.

Brushing against its corner, I went behind the wood backstop of the baseball field. The backstop was solid. I went flat on the dirt and tried to remember what brought me there. It seemed I'd been there before, trying to remember what had brought me there. A voice came from my half hand. I looked toward the voice and saw a peculiar object that emitted, "Jeff. Jeff? Can you hear me?"

Inez. I put the phone to my lips. Like the backstop, it was solid. "I need help."

"What's wrong?"

Pale colors swirled the air like a river eddy. "I don't know."

"Are you incredibly drunk? Like skunk drunk?"

"I've been drugged. Psychedelics."

Inez's voice kicked up a notch. "Where are you?"

"Forester Park. I'm hiding behind the baseball backstop."

"Why?"

"Life is a joke played on us by the gods. Now mine's about to be over. I want to try again. I know I can do better."

Inez said, "Promise me you won't move."

"Nothing's real. We think it is, but life's a mammoth joke."

"I'm not a joke. I'll drop Bianca next door and be on my way."

"On what way?"

"Jeff, stay there. Stay where you are."

In wood bleachers the two nuns in white cloaks skimmed fingers across shiny rosary beads, and recited separate prayers. The slow blinking, darkness to faded colors, persisted. Mesmerized, I watched the colored air in front of me move in slow circles. It seemed I'd been there and watched air move in circles before. It seemed important to remember another time I'd hidden behind the wood backstop watching colored air puff around in time with my breaths.

I heard a car park on the street, one of its doors open and close. I'd forgotten Inez was coming. In the slow-blinking murkiness, she dragged me by an arm, packed me onto the backseat of her Nissan. Door locks clacked.

"Are you taking me to where the joke ends?"

"You're going home. Miller Drive. Do you know that's where you live?"

"It doesn't matter. Everything's a joke played on us."

Inez's voice floated in the car. "You'll be fine once the drugs wash through."

"How do you care about things once you know they're not real?"

"First," Inez said, "we get you home. We can work on the rest."

"I don't know if I believe you."

"That's okay. We're getting you home."

Thirteen

My head throbbed. A bamboo window blind was lowered in the tiny bedroom. Sunlight seeped through. In the room were the narrow bed that barely held me, a side table with a lamp, a doorless closet thirty-six inches wide. Nothing more. Thoughts were slow to form. I had no memory of getting into bed.

My mind stitched images together. Colored water arcing from sprinklers. Nuns on a baseball infield. The wood backstop. Inez pulling me to her car. All of it came in separate portions, unconnected.

"Ine?" It came out squeaky. I spoke louder. "Ine? Are you here?"

I swung legs over the edge of the bed, stood and immediately plopped back onto the mattress. No strength in the legs.

Inez appeared in the open doorway. She scooted along the tight lane at the side of the mattress and handed me a glass of water. I emptied the glass, gave it back.

"What time is it?" I asked.

"Eight-thirty." I was given a visual check-up, like you do with a patient who wanders in from the street. "Do you know where you are?"

I nodded.

Inez's face looked like she hadn't slept much, if at all. She seemed to choose her words carefully. "You suffered a psychotic episode last night. Are you aware of that?"

I nodded again.

"Let's get you out of this room, see where you're at."

Gazing around, things were familiar yet somehow changed. "Okay."

I stood with my hands against the wall. Sliding sideways on the sheetrock, I made it to the doorway. Inez got behind me, grabbed my hips and guided me to stretching out on the long brown couch. I wore a gray T-shirt and Jockey shorts. Inez must have found them and put them on me. I massaged my thudding forehead. This made me wonder if whatever psychedelic was slipped into the water was laced with something noxious.

Inez sat in the chair across from me, on the other side of the coffee table. "How much do you remember?"

"Fragments. Going bonkers in Forester Park. Don't remember calling you, do remember hearing your voice. I remember being in the car, feeling wet clothes sticking to me. Not much after."

Inez brought me a glass of orange juice, asked if I thought I could eat something. While she fried an egg and made toast, I drank orange juice and began piecing together images from the moment the food at Homer's Café pulsed orange and amber. It was analogous to gazing down a lengthy train tunnel. A plate was set in front of me on the coffee table, egg on toast, with a fork. I nibbled at the egg on toast.

Inez sat across from me in the armchair. "Do you remember

saying life is a joke? That nothing's real. You got worked up about it."

Another bite. The cobwebs were slowly dispersing. "What we think of as our life," I said, "is all projections. I've had those thoughts before. Last night I experienced it. Lived it."

Inez's exhausted face didn't droop or relax. "You were out of your mind for a few hours."

She went to the kitchen, poured herself a glass of orange juice and returned to the plum-colored chair. "Do you remember calling me Karen?"

"No. Sorry."

Inez drank orange juice. She smiled wanly. "I learned a lot about you last night. Do you mind if we talk about it?"

"I don't think I'm in a position to mind anything. You saved me."

Inez said I'd confessed to being the catalyst behind a man named David Gummer driving drunk from Reno to Fallen Leaf Lake, near Lake Tahoe, where my ex-wife Karen and I then lived. I'd humiliated Gummer twice, first by knocking him around in his office, then that night toying with him—and he pissed his pants in the presence of a woman he had minutes before declared his love for. A couple of days later, Gummer shot a window in our cabin, obviously to scare Karen and me. He'd dashed to his car, and while racing away ran head-on into a police car driven by an officer on his way to protect us. Both men died instantly.

"You said it's only in the last year you've come to understand you ruined, quote, 'our' marriage to punish yourself. To punish yourself for causing two men to die young. You started drinking heavily again, like after your hand got cut. And withdrew from everyone, including Karen. Especially Karen, spending most of your time alone. You said you grew up pretty much alone in the woods. That basketball was the only thing that got you mixing with other people."

I didn't remember telling Inez any of that, but it was all true. "That's right. It's wrapped up into my hesitation, with us. I always screw things up. And when I do, think of the message about men that would send Bianca. After her dad already walked out on her."

"Why can't you give yourself a break? Whatever you did wrong, it was years ago."

I looked to the palms of my hands, remembered watching the pores breathe. Remembered the miracle of it.

Inez finished her orange juice and set the empty glass on the coffee table. She gave me another looking over. "If you're sure you're going to be okay, I'll go home for some sleep. If I stay here, I'll just worry."

"I'll be okay. I'm just still dopey."

"One more thing. Who do you think did it?"

"No idea. It was probably a random prank."

Not true. I had a candidate. Odin. He was the only person who might have a motive to mess with my head. And he knew of my Sunday dinners at Homer's Café. I tried to remember what other people there had looked like, and came up empty. I'd had no reason to pay close attention to the other diners.

Inez came around behind the couch and kissed me on a cheek. "We'll talk later. Any paranoia, like last night, call me pronto."

Overwhelmed by shaky pictures of the night before, I fell into a light sleep. I slept off and on all morning.

Inez called. She asked if I thought it was okay if she went into work. I said I'd be fine. At saying goodbye, I almost told Inez I loved her, but wasn't certain I knew anything about love.

Thinking it would be good to get outside, I walked along Miller Drive and over to Forester Park. The sunlight seemed harsh. At the park's upper end, greenery behind me, I sat on a wood bench and tried to make sense of what had happened. My brain was getting better at raising images, though I still couldn't put them into a coherent re-creation of the night before.

At the park's center, kids played on swings, rocking horses, climbing structures. Two men walking an asphalt path together stared at their phones. Moms and a few dads chatted. Children swooped around, chattering like birds. Everyone seemed happy. They didn't understand that none of it was real. They didn't know life is a joke played on us by the gods.

A small white butterfly, of the same size as those in Edwina's drawing, landed atop the other end of the bench. Its petite wings arose in tandem, and sealed together overhead. The butterfly looked at me. I was sure of it. Or was the butterfly another mental projection? I scooted across the bench and flicked my hand toward the butterfly. It didn't move. I flicked my hand again. The same non-result. Walking home, I decided not to tell Inez about it.

Fourteen

Tuesday at work nobody asked about Monday's absence, which meant Inez had told everyone not to. I was living two lives. One was an endless cycle of trying to find existential truths in what I'd experienced. The other was getting back to focusing on what I'd spent years training for, to help others with their health. Days passed. The world gradually seemed more like it had been, filled with scenic landscapes I enjoyed, and people I engaged with. Like Shannon Lunge.

"I'm finishing up inside work at Moran's," he said. "There's your name on the notepad. It's got a big X across it. I worried you might, you know, not be okay."

"I don't know what you're talking about. How's the BP been?"

Shannon sat on the padded beige examining table, white T-shirt sleeves rolled up. He shrugged and offered his left arm. I engaged the cuff, and read numbers as it tightened.

"You ain't got much of a poker face," Shannon said. "You know more about your name being up there than you're saying."

"Quiet. Relax."

After I deflated the cuff, and turned to put away the instrument, Shannon said, "What're this week's lotto numbers?"

"One forty-two over ninety-three. Not good B.P., but better."

"Hey, got my taxes in on time. Didn't have to pay as much as I thought. Maybe it took a load off."

I instructed Shannon to take slow, deep breaths, and listened to his lungs. When I was done, Shannon hopped down from the examining table.

"You got me curious about this Moran guy," I said. "His name keeps popping up. What goes on at his place, anyway?"

"A lot of people coming and going. Some look shady as hell. What they're up to, I can't say. Moran has these moose-size twins that act as muscle. I don't see why he needs them, but they live up there."

"You say they're twins?" I had wondered about that.

"Bam and Sam Branford. Took me a while to tell them apart. They're killer types."

The door burst open. A man about forty, long dark hair wild, eyes a burning liquid gray, charged in. His brown hair hung in matted gobs, like it hadn't been washed or combed in weeks. A purple scar ran from below the left eye down his cheek and onto his neck. Robin shouted from the front desk, telling him he couldn't just bust in anywhere he wanted. He could because in his arms he cradled a woman of roughly his age. At her right hand was a washcloth crudely wrapped in loops of duct tape.

Shannon hopped off the exam table, looked to the eyes-blazing man. "Woodrow," he said.

The man deposited the woman on the table. His reddened face seemed about to explode with fire. He directed that heat at me. "Fix her or I'll hurt you. I'll hurt you bad."

Robin appeared at the door, eyes agape. "What should I–"

I motioned for her to stop, so I could concentrate on the desperate-looking arrivals.

The woman had tangled frizzy blonde hair. She wore jeans blanched of color, and a faintly green top. She appeared as weathered as her clothes. Wary of her escort, I went to her. She opened her eyes. Her pupils were dilated. She smelled of sweat and cannabis.

Lips trembling, she said, "The bucket."

The man's face flashed shock. He let go of the woman and barely avoided colliding with Robin at fleeing. He crashed through the clinic's lobby, knocking over folding chairs. A door opened and slammed against the outside wall of the old building.

Shrieks and buzzing chatter came from the lobby. To Robin, Shannon said, "Excuse me." He started down the hallway. His voice carried across Yates Health. "It's all right. Nothing to worry about. Stay calm, take your seats. Thank you for your cooperation."

Blood oozed from the crude bandage. I got the patient flat on her back, asked her to open her eyes. Her pupils were exceptionally dilated; still, her eyes followed the movements of the old fashioned pen light I used with patients. Storm came into the room.

"Take her," I said. This allowed me to rush into the hallway, and call to Shannon. "Find him. Don't touch him but keep track of him."

"Got it."

I spun around, went back to the patient. "No pain meds yet," I said. "We need to know everything she's on."

Storm nodded as he looked her over. "Agreed."

Shannon yelled down the hall. "He's comin' back! He's comin' back!"

To Robin, I said, "Lock yourself in my office."

Storm began to carefully unwind duct tape off the washcloth bandage. The chaos of the moment did not affect him. I held the woman steady. Inez entered the room, watched what was happening.

"We okay?"

"So far," I said.

Storm said, "If he brings in a pipe or something, I'll get his legs. Grab his wrist and bite his hand off."

The man surged through the doorway, head snapping like a fish out of water. He held a dirty steel bucket chest high, located me and thrust the steel bucket at my gut. "Put 'em back on. Put 'em back good or I'll hurt you."

Soon as I grasped the bucket, the man fled again. I looked down. Two half fingers were seen through chunks of ice.

Inez said, "What is it?"

"Fingers. Two." To Storm, I said, "Bring the ambulance around. We're not waiting for a chopper. We'll beat it if we leave right now."

Storm reflexively patted pockets.

Inez said, "Top drawer of Robin's desk." She held the woman's arm, the bloody ragged bandage crowning it. "I'll call Memorial. Let's get going."

Storm jogged down the hallway. He and Shannon crossed by each other without a word.

Shannon, short of breath, came into the now-crowded examining room. "He's out in a school bus. I seen him go in."

Sandy Lewis arrived, stethoscope around her neck. "I'll take vitals." She took the woman's free hand and felt for a pulse.

"Then get her to the exit," I said. "Shannon, you carry. The ambulance will pull up in front. You and Storm get her in." I turned to Inez. "If I'm not out of the bus within a minute after she's situated, go without me."

Outside, parked crookedly in front of the Yates Health entrance, was an old yellow school bus spackled with dried mud. The name of the school district it once belonged to was covered with squiggly lines of black spray paint. A few townsfolk had gathered.

"In there," said a man. "He's hella-crazy."

I worked open the bus's folding door, climbed inside, dipped my head to accommodate the roof line. Behind the driver's seat were two rows of padded bench seats on each side. Beyond them was a mix of blankets, a bare mattress and cardboard boxes. Piled in a corner were a black wet suit, mask, snorkel and a spear gun. There was no time for introductions or niceties. I tore the blanket off a human-sized lump. The man brandished a buck knife.

"Get your ass back."

"Is she your significant other?"

"What about it?"

"We need you for information. Any time you waste here will go against success in treating her."

"I ain't going in 'til they fix her. They got machines in there that read your mind."

I reached out my half hand, stopping inches before the gleaming knife. The man stared at the stumps where I'd once had fingers. He, like the woman he'd brought to the clinic, was stoned. He tipped his head, taking in the diminished hand, and dropped the knife. I grabbed his arm and yanked him upright as hard as I could.

He tried to free his arm from my grasp. "Them machines invade your head. They're mind parasites."

"We're taking your lady friend to Santa Rosa. You want to be with her or be left behind?"

I pushed the man outside. He rose an arm to block sun glare; people moved away. Ahead, Storm Elliot was at the wheel of a boxy white ambulance. Its back doors were open.

Seeing us, Inez climbed out. "Sandy called Memorial. They'll try to get their best hands guy there ahead of you."

"Is she out?"

"Sandy gave her a little help," Inez said. "Before she wrapped the hand tighter."

The man with a long purple face scar looked to the gurney inside. The woman was strapped to it. He got in swiftly. I followed. The siren wailed. The man pressed hands over his ears and squeezed his eyes shut. Inez slammed the rear doors.

Storm shouted, "The chairs have seat belts. Use them."

Storm's years on motorcycles surely enhanced his skills as an ambulance driver. Once out of Yates and on the twisty road to Appleton, he employed the flashing red lights, not the siren; Storm later explained that coming around a tight bend with the siren blaring could cause a driver to crash.

The gurney filled most of one side. On the other side, the wild man and I sat strapped in chairs four feet apart.

The man, eyes burning redder than I'd ever seen, answered

my questions. His name: Rick Fulton. The woman zonked out in the gurney: Kim Johnson. They lived off the grid in the sparsely populated ridges to the northwest. He didn't specify where. I asked what drugs Kim had taken.

"One of the tranqs the V.A. gives me at my annual exam. I mean tranquilizers."

"What else?"

Rick shook his head *no.*

"I'm not the cops. We need to know what's in her. You're both bombed."

Rick thought it over. "We traded for some new-ass pot grown by this mad scientist up by Laytonville. Two hits, and we're like flying carpets. I went inside to lie down. I guess Kim decided to chop kindling. I didn't know. I would've stopped her."

I ran a hand down the left side of my face, indicating his curved purple scar. "Cause?"

The ambulance sped onward.

Rick pointed to my half hand. "You first."

I described an accident that occurred the summer after I graduated from Sacramento State, working the tomato harvest. How I'd daydreamed my way into losing the two fingers and half of a third.

"What's it like to live with?"

"For years it was bad, because I couldn't quit thinking about it. Now it just is. Kim's hand won't look anything like mine. Not remotely close."

In the back of the ambulance was a small square window. Strips of blue sky were followed by shadows that whizzed past. Storm's driving never made the tires skid. I noted that Kim didn't resist the heaving motions the rushing ambulance put her body through even though she was strapped down.

I fingered my cheek again. "Your turn."

"Second Iraq. Disarming roadside bombs. I did everything like they trained us. The screen showed clear. Ran the sequence twice. My buddy goes to drive ahead. He's blown to bits, and I got this." Dirty fingers touched the purple scar. "It was Kim saved me." Rick stared at her with such anguish, and devotion, I reached over and squeezed his arm. His voice grew faint. "We were only friends when I signed up. When they shipped me stateside, she let me move into her apartment. I drove her roommate out in like a week. You think I'm bad now? You should've seen me the first few years."

"I don't think you're bad. I think you're hurting."

Chin down, not looking my way, Rick extended his right hand. I shook it with my left.

The ambulance slowed. Storm smacked the horn a few times. "Wake up! Can't you see the lights?" He hit the horn again. "Goddamn you!"

Rick looked over at me. I shrugged. Rick unfastened his seat belt, went to the floor, and lost his balance when the ambulance made a turn.

"You can't touch her," I said.

"She keeps me from losing it. I'll touch her elbow." Rick wiped his mouth. "Just her elbow."

"For a couple seconds, no more. Don't make me pull you away. Kim could get hurt."

Rick grabbed the metal gurney railing with one hand, to steady himself. He touched Kim on the elbow of her left arm.

Her right, with the taped washcloth, was secured at her other side. Since the cause of the accident was a hand axe, this told me Kim was left-handed. If nothing else, she'd always have use of her better coordinated hand.

Rick whispered, "Kim Love," and ran fingertips in a slow circle over her skin. Rick kissed the tip of his index finger and touched it to Kim's elbow. He crawled backwards, waited for the ambulance to advance on a straight stretch, got seated and fastened the seatbelt.

Rick said, "Where are we?"

"Outskirts of Appleton. Get ready. Once we hit Highway 12 he'll use the siren again."

Rick bobbed with the movements of the ambulance. He reached between us and fanned his fingers. "Where are they?"

Fitted into the side wall, left of Rick, was a stainless-steel box, a kind of freezer with a door that looked like a microwave oven's. Small red lights blinked across the bottom of the frame. I pointed to it.

"We'll get them to the docs. They'll do their best."

Rick looked at the freezer device. "Fuckin' machines are everywhere," he said.

Fifteen

A waiting room occupied the opposite end of the hall from the surgery center. Stocked with the usual magazines, a bible and cloth armchairs sporting cheerful colors, it was far enough from the operating theater to discourage family members from trying to communicate with staff coming or going. The room had a wide opening in place of a door. Rick sat hunched in a corner chair. His forehead pressed the wall. I resisted an impulse to take out my phone and check messages.

I contemplated the coincidence of my two sliced-off fingers and Rick and Kim showing up with two half fingers in a bucket of ice. Or was it a coincidence? Ever since meeting Edwina, my thinking about how life worked had been thrown into question. I was both sure of almost nothing, and open to the thought that anything was possible.

Maybe there was such a thing as fate.

The sound of approaching footsteps. A man wearing glasses and nurse's blues, stopped in the opening to the waiting room. A blue face mask clung to his Adam's apple. One look at Rick and he knew which of us was with the patient.

I stood, and had my half hand in a jeans pocket before the man could be distracted by it.

With Rick's head lodged in the corner, the man spoke to me. "I'm Dr. Henry. And you are?"

"Dr. Taylor. Yates Health. I accompanied Mr. Fulton in the ambulance. He and the patient came to us in their emergency."

Dr. Henry looked over my work wardrobe with either puzzlement or disdain: a long-sleeved button-down work shirt, worn jeans, running shoes. That and working at Yates Health didn't place me in an upper echelon of Sonoma County's medical community.

Rick turned away from the wall. His face red as ever, he said, "Is her hand going to be okay? Don't you dare bullshit me."

A smile, coolly professional, from Dr. Henry. "I came to tell you it will be another hour or so."

"Can't you hear? I asked if she's going to be okay."

Another practiced smile. "We won't know today, or tomorrow, or next week. It takes months to estimate how far a patient may eventually progress. I can tell you this. Dr. Wun is as skilled a hand surgeon as anyone north of the Golden Gate Bridge. Long and short, we're doing everything we can."

Rick spread his angry red heat. "If it turns out you put a tracking device in her, I'm coming after you. I got your name. It's Dr. Henry. I'll find you. Don't think I won't."

Dr. Henry said goodbye and walked down the hallway.

I went to Rick and put my face next to his. Voice low, I growled, "We got Kim here quick and safe. She has a good surgeon. What you do now is, you sit, you wait, and you show some respect. Do I make myself clear?"

Rick turned his face to the wall. "I'm scared, man. She's my whole world."

"I get it. Hang in there."

I returned to my seat, picked up an old copy of *Sports Illustrated*, and tried to read. My purpose in staying there was to be sure Rick didn't crash into the operating theater. The clock showed three p.m. A male nurse led a couple into the waiting area. They were about Rick's age, or younger, and shared his fashion sense and an indifference to bathing. At seeing me they flinched and sent each other a momentary look of surprise. Then introduced themselves as Joan and Jim Finnegan. I kept the half hand out of sight.

At hearing the names, Rick looked up. "How'd you find out?"

"Sam Dowd called," Jim said. "He saw the bus in Yates, asked people what went down."

Joan went to Rick, who got out of the chair. She gave him a fulsome hug. Rick didn't let go.

Jim said, "Hey, I get a turn."

This brought a feeble smile to Rick's scarred face. He and Jim wiggled side-to-side in their lengthy hug, and Jim pulled Rick to another chair, so he sat between his two friends.

"They're neighbors," Rick said. "Like a mile down the mountain."

"We watch out for each other," Jim said.

Joan touched Rick on the arm. "How's it look?"

Rick tipped his head toward me, and held hands with both Finnegans. "He's a doctor."

I told them what I knew, which wasn't much. Jim and Joan assured Rick that Kim was going to be all right.

"She's stubborn," Joan said. "She'll work those fingers back into action. You'll see."

Rick didn't seem convinced.

Jim stood, stepped to me and offered a hand. "We can take it from here. Thanks for helping out."

"You've been super," Joan said.

In the middle of the handshake, Jim looked down. "Whoa."

Joan said, "*Jimbo*. Jesus."

"No worries. I'm used to it." I took a business card from my wallet and handed it to Rick. "If you need something, call any time. That's my direct number."

I didn't make it through the room's opening before Rick clobbered me from the side with a running bear hug. "You're good people," he said.

Outside, I called an Uber. I wasn't eager to return to Yates Health. It would be abuzz with the day's drama. I'd spend the rest of the afternoon answering questions. I checked my phone. No messages from Inez. The Uber car arrived. I opened a rear door and climbed in.

"Luther Burbank's house."

The Luther Burbank Home and Gardens sat approximately in the center of Santa Rosa. I'd never seen a relatively modest space as filled with close to its array of plants and trees. Afternoon sun drew various scents from evergreen trees and bright flowers. There was a greenhouse with angled sides of overlapping panes. Open space contained a swishing, stone-backed fountain that fed a large pool with underwater growth. A pair of scarlet dragon flies buzzed over the pond like planes in formation.

There were two, two-story, white wood structures. One had been Luther Burbank's home. The other, formerly a carriage house, was home to memorabilia, dozens of old photographs, books, postcards and posters of flowers and fruits created via Burbank's various graftings.

A trim woman in crisp blue jeans and a man's white dress shirt presided over a counter at one end of the converted space. On the counter were pamphlets and a credit card reader. The woman's black hair fell in a neat upside-down bowl. She had bright hazel eyes. On the wall behind her were memorabilia. On her shirt rode a gold pin with "Marj" printed on it in black.

I wandered the large room. One piece of memorabilia struck me like a hammer's blow: a colored pencil drawing of a small cottage, fronted by richly colored flowers. An exquisite, detailed drawing.

I approached the counter.

Marj gifted me a disarming smile. "May I help you?"

"That drawing." I pointed. "Did Luther Burbank make it?"

"You've hit on our mystery. In his effects, Mr. Burbank didn't leave anything else remotely resembling this. Many years ago, the association hired an expert who established the date of execution as between 1920 and 1940. It's not signed or initialed."

Marj had my rapt attention.

She said, "That's the cottage at Mr. Burbank's Experiment Farm, in Appleton. Are you familiar with it?"

"It's an interesting place."

"About forty years ago—no, more now," Marj said, "people got together and did a great job out there with what had become a tangle of vegetation. They're good folks. Anyway, they'd like to have our drawing. But it was found here, in a trunk, when Mrs. Burbank passed away decades after he did. She was thirty-nine years younger than her husband. Sorry." Marj inclined her head forward. "Us Burbankers tend to get obsessed with details. I hope I'm not boring you."

"Not at all. I'm curious if you have any clues, even a wild guess, as to who drew the picture."

My eyes didn't leave the drawing, comparing it to the one I'd bought and the two others I'd seen. This one was somewhat faded, yet the overall visual effect reminded me distinctly of Edwina's creations.

Marj slowly shook her head. "We've tried to find out. It's a complete mystery. What's interesting about that," Marj added, "is there are few mysteries in Mr. Burbank's story. It has been thoroughly chronicled."

We were the only people in the former carriage house. My eyes examined the cottage drawing long enough to make Marj openly uncomfortable. She stepped in front of it. I got the hint, thanked her and slipped a five-dollar bill into a clear plastic box with a slot for donations.

Outside, I hailed another Uber.

Heading west, a text from Inez arrived, asking where I was. *Heading to yates will fill you in.*

Sixteen

I paid with the app, waved to the driver, and got out. The day's warmth had diminished. Gray clouds drifted overhead. At the other end of town, flashing police lights caught my eye. Orange cones were in the street, corralling traffic into a slim lane. An officer directed traffic. It was a good excuse to further delay going back to work. I walked toward two police cars, with open space between them. About ten people watched the goings on from an adjacent driveway. Beyond the secured area, redwood trees hugged the road. Shadows hovered between them.

One of the gawkers, Bill Rothman, forty-seven years old, had recently come to the clinic with a painful cough. He had been exposed to asbestos in his late teens, working construction for a home remodeling company. Thankfully, it turned out Bill had pleurisy. He saw me coming, touched his chest and gave a thumbs up.

I reached him. "What happened?"

Bill's red hair hung in ringlets. He grimaced and smiled simultaneously. Blue eyes peered between the twirled hair. "A woman's walking into town with her kid. Like a three-year-old boy. She's on her phone. The kid wanders into the road."

Bill's smile surpassed the grimace. He was visibly excited. "Mom's too busy yakking to notice the kid's gone. Out of nowhere," Bill said, and jerked a thumb over his shoulder, "a woman comes running off Duncan's Valley Trail. Like at full speed. Runs straight into the street. No way to grab the kid, so she throws herself in front of a car. She gets smushed when the driver swerves and barely misses the boy."

A woman a few feet over, eyes wide, said, "It was like a self-sacrifice. Think of the guts it took."

"Did you see it?"

"No. It's what everybody's saying."

Suddenly nauseous, I said goodbye and walked to the cordoned off area. An older officer, arms folded across his chest, surveyed the work of an investigative crew. His gray face had deep wrinkles at the sides of his eyes. He scraped his teeth with a toothpick.

"Excuse me?" I raised a hand, like I had a question.

The man removed the toothpick. "Don't step over the tape. I'll come to you."

He came. I extended my right hand. The man tucked the toothpick between his lips. Something about his eyes brought to mind the phrase *seen it all*. His teeth, like the rest of him, seemed whittled by time.

"I'm with Yates Health. I understand there was an accident. Any needs here?"

"No." Seeing my half hand while shaking it, the officer said, "So you're Dr. Taylor. I'm told you make West County rounds, too. I'm told you'll go anywhere, any hour."

"You saying you make West County rounds means you're the man people call Mayor Carbone."

The toothpick was plucked, dropped to the pavement. "They call me that because I handle much of the area. Had the same territory for thirty-eight years."

In front of me, in thick dark-blue uniforms, wearing sky-blue surgical gloves, was a woman photographer and a man making notes. He slowly walked an area that had a chalk body outline and three miniature yellow marker flags. There were black skid marks. No rubble was scattered on the pavement.

"I understand it was a hit and run."

"Fatality," Carbone said. "A young woman, I'm guessing middle twenties. Driver—witness says she thinks male. Caucasian. He hits her and keeps going. The son of a bitch killed her and just kept going."

I almost asked what the victim looked like, then thought better of it.

"Someone from around here? I might know her from the clinic."

His eyes watchful, Carbone said, "Never seen her before. No I.D. on her. We whisked everyone awa— Wait, do you know what happened, doctor?"

"I heard a boy went into the street while Mom's on her phone. A good Samaritan rushes out in front of the vehicle, so the car won't hit the child. Any info on the car?"

Carbone snapped the fingers of his right hand. "Happened like that. All we got is a big dark vehicle. Maybe black. Not a pickup."

My quick thought: One of Moran's thugs, or Moran himself. The second thought: The roads were filled with big dark SUVs.

Carbone turned to answer a question, in a low voice, posed by the woman officer. I couldn't make out their exchange. Carbone turned to me.

"The driver comes down Graton Road, slides through the stop sign and guns it onto Bohemian. We took the mother, the boy, and the only witness, a woman walking into town for groceries, to the Guerneville substation. Remove them from the trauma scene, for follow up."

"Did you get a specialist to communicate with the boy?"

"That's procedure."

I thought of asking about the witness. Maybe I could talk to her. A crazy idea. I figured I'd better shut up before Carbone caught on to my heightened interest in events.

"Good to meet you," I said. "Hope you catch the driver."

Carbone said, "We should have coffee. If you're going to be doctoring on my roads, we should get to know each other."

I said that was a good idea, and walked to downtown. I cut around behind Yates Health, got into my car and drove up and then along Duncan's Valley Road. That the victim hadn't carried identification weighed on me. When I reached the dirt road that led down to SunSpot, two cars were parked on the slope. I walked downhill in an indirect way, stopping a few times, listening for other people, not wanting to be seen.

I crawled through the thicket tunnel, jogged to the blue tarp. "Edwina, it's Jeff. Are you there?"

No answer.

"Edwina, if you're there, please let me know. It's important."

Of course she wasn't there. I already knew but was still half in denial. Carefully, as though not wanting to disturb anything, I unhooked the tarp, curled forward, entered and fell to my knees.

The light was low. I saw well enough to know nothing had changed. The truth of Edwina's death expanded inside me. I settled on the tan blankets and drew them to my lips, as a comfort. Edwina had peacefully waited for whatever she'd been sent to do. The enormity of knowing her, and its implications regarding the nature of existence, was outside my ability to comprehend. I turned onto my side and curled into the fetal position.

Overwhelmed by sudden loss, I drifted in a state that felt subterranean—and broke from that state of mind. I needed to search the tree-trunk abode for any references to me. If they were discovered, I couldn't imagine talking to the police about the time spent with Edwina. I used my phone's light to help search through Edwina's orderly things.

In a folder was the note containing my contact information; a drawing of looking down at the tight valley of old-growth redwoods; a pen and ink drawing of my diminished hand.

I took the drawings, the page with my contact information and the envelope it was in, and left the tree-trunk house. I set the material aside, notched the tarp to redwood bark and walked uphill in dim light. The drive to Appleton was trance-like. It was hard to pay attention to the roads.

Parked outside of Inez's modest wood house on James Street, in old Appleton, I felt empty inside. Hollow, like an egg emptied of the life inside it. I couldn't decide whether or not to call Inez. Night came. Still I sat, numbed by loss. There were no streetlights. No sidewalks. Trees in every yard. Light from the house next door spread over asphalt. A dark cat, crouched, eyes shining against the light, looked my way. Then it tip-toed across the road.

I tapped my phone.

Inez's voice came fast. "Where have you been?"

"When I got back to Yates, I saw police cars. I learned about the woman getting killed in a hit and run. It sent me over the edge. I've been driving around."

"Where are you now?"

"In my car, in front of your house."

"Why don't you come to the door?"

"I don't know."

"You're a strange one, Jeff Taylor."

"I think I just got stranger."

Bianca was still awake, which helped. We played her favorite card game, Rat-A-Tat-Cat. Unlike wall ball, there was no need to go easy. Bianca's hands moved fast, and she won the majority of the games.

When Inez and Bianca went down the hall for bedtime reading, I raided the refrigerator. Its door was covered with Bianca's artwork. I wolfed down sliced chicken on bread. Beer or wine did not appeal. I drank tap water and looked around the 1930s redwood house painted a deep, marine green outside and the boards left rough inside. Pine shelves were lined with ceramic teacups, no two alike. Lots of books, half for children. Shoes off, I stretched out on a futon couch.

Inez returned. She made two cups of peppermint tea, and sat next to me on the couch. We took sips. The warm tea felt good going down.

"The women who got hit," Inez said, "was she the Teacher

Lady Bianca talked about? I heard she came down from the trail not wearing shoes."

"Yes."

"I believed you when you said you weren't seeing someone else."

"Because it's true. Bianca's Teacher Lady was homeless. I thought delusional. So I helped her out. I brought her food. Things she needed."

"For example?"

"Colored pencils. Good drawing paper. She made drawings she sold at Yates General. That's what she lived on."

Inez picked up her tea, took a sip. "So you were being Mr. Nice Guy, merely helping her out."

"She helped me more than I helped her."

"How is that possible?"

"By how she was. By some of the things she said. It's hard to explain. It wouldn't sound interesting now."

"Was she good looking?"

"Let me be clear. I never even brushed against her skin." My voice grew loud. "I touch people all day, every day. It never crossed my mind if she was good looking or not."

"Why didn't you tell me about this?"

"Because you'd tell me to take the situation to professionals. I mean, you're my boss in that arena. I thought an intervention— she'd be forced to leave the woods—could do more harm than good. She seemed happy living like a hermit. Happier and saner than most people."

Inez shook her head. As was her habit when under stress, she combed fingers back through her dark hair.

"You saying you got stranger, is it because of her death?"

"Because of her life. Because of her death."

Inez grabbed her knees. She closed her eyes, pursed her lips. "I think you're going through a psychological crisis. Maybe the breakup with Karen is finally hitting home. Something that major can be buried for years. When it bursts forth, it's devastating. I think you getting drugged may have burst open the dam."

I sipped tea. Considered telling Inez I knew what I'd done was unorthodox. That Bianca's Teacher Lady was unlike anyone I'd ever encountered, and it had affected my judgment. That my habit was to think I knew better than others when it came to helping people in need.

Instead, I took the easy way out. "You're right. Wrecking things with Karen screwed me up in ways I'm only now beginning to understand."

This was true, but secondary to my grieving. And not for a second did I consider telling Inez that the woman she referred to as Teacher Lady, Edwina Seeba, was some kind of spirit who from time to time returned to earth.

PART TWO

Seventeen

MYSTERY WOMAN KILLED IN ACCIDENT was the next morning's front page all caps headline in the *Daily Democrat*. Below it was a photograph of the accident scene, with police officers going about their work. Right of that was a map with dotted lines showing the end point of Edwina's sprint, with question marks placed here and there along Duncan's Valley Trail. After a brief account of the hit and run, Mystery Woman's selfless act was praised by elected officials, including Sonoma County Sheriff Edward Pierce, West County supervisor Nanette Hapkins, and in letters to the editor. Every article I found online contained a request asking readers to report any information they had about Mystery Woman, or the hit and run, to the sheriff's department.

Edwina's running barefoot from where the trail dropped into town to in front of a speeding vehicle gave the tragedy an exotic, even mythic quality. No photographs of the victim were released. She'd carried no identification. Fingerprints and DNA samples yielded nothing.

"She could be anyone, from anywhere," Sheriff Pierce announced at a press conference. "Possibly from another country. We're looking down every avenue. I again ask anyone who knew her, or think they knew this hero, to contact the Sonoma County Sheriff's Department. We are hoping to inform her family of her passing."

Inez, aware of my peculiar emotional state, didn't confront me. Still, if I didn't go to the authorities, she rightly would. Plus, I'd told Kurt Sanderson at Yates General I'd met the woman who made precise botanical drawings. It was reasonable to assume he'd pass that along. Though having done nothing illegal, I was wary of talking to the police.

I had no choice.

An afternoon voice message netted a prompt call from a Lieutenant Don Wills. He suggested in a manner that wasn't really asking that we meet at seven p.m., at department headquarters in Santa Rosa.

Wills greeted me at glass entry doors. He wore a short-sleeved shirt, jeans, and running shoes. He had brown eyes and marine-cut brown hair. His dark mustache was pencil thin in accordance with his physique. He'd done his homework and didn't show surprise at shaking hands.

Few people were in the building at that hour. We walked along a hallway that exuded a barren administrative sensation I would not have experienced before the night Inez plucked me from the dirt at Forester Park. Since then, all feelings were amplified by a more acute perception of everything around me.

"I'll take notes," Wills said, "but I consider this an informal interview. Any information you can give us will be appreciated."

Wills invited me to enter a small office. He closed the door. On the one desk was a framed picture of himself and who I assumed to be his wife, two young daughters and a German Shepard larger than the children. In the background were a home swing set and a fence that looked new.

Wills asked if he could tape our conversation. I consented. He got his iPhone ready, set it on his metal desk. He spoke his name, rank, and who he worked for, followed by the date, time and location of the interview.

"Do you have any reason to believe you should have an attorney present?"

If that was his idea of informal, I figured formal was tossing someone in the back of a squad car.

"I don't need a lawyer."

"Just trying to head off potential complications. Were you on the receiving end of any threat, or suggestion of consequences, if you didn't come in and share what you are about to tell me?"

"No."

Wills opened a notebook, held a pen an inch above a lined page.

"What do you know about the woman who was killed in a hit and run near the corner of Graton Road and Bohemian Highway? Yesterday afternoon. Anything that comes to mind. It doesn't matter whether it seems relevant or not."

I launched into my memorized tale. Described Bianca getting lost when playing hide and seek. Bianca's telling me a Teacher Lady guided her up the correct trail. Next was believing the woman was homeless—no shoes, wandering the woodlands in a dress—and how that led to thinking I should check on her. Next came the first lie, saying I went to SunSpot and Teacher Lady emerged from trees and we talked on the flat area up on top. I described bringing her food, and colored pencils and paper for her drawings, sales of which provided her livelihood.

The wood of the chair I sat in seemed to poke me between the shoulder blades.

"It became a Sunday ritual," I said. "Checking to be sure she was okay before going to the beach for a run. That was about it. I didn't see any indication living out there was doing her harm. She seemed stable, happy. She seemed good."

Wills nodded. He cleared his throat. "Were you two ever intimate?"

"I literally never touched her. We'd talk maybe ten minutes. She'd say thanks for whatever I brought, and disappear down one trail or another. My guess is she returned at night, when no one was around, and slept in one of the SunSpot structures. They'd provide protection from the elements. That was my guess, because nights can get cold and foggy out there."

Wills scribbled words, stopped. "Go on."

"I've dealt with a fair amount of homeless folks. I've found it's better not to push things. Let them open up to you. In the long run, that's the most effective way to help them."

"What was her appearance? What did she look like?"

I described Edwina slowly, as if she weren't clear in my mind.

"When did you first hear of our request for information?"

"I watched the news conference last night."

"Why didn't you contact us? Why the wait until this afternoon?"

Shifting in the chair, I took a slow, deep breath, a remnant of my basketball days, standing at the free throw line before taking a shot.

"Lieutenant, we're having financial difficulties at Yates Health. That's why I didn't call right away."

Wills gave his thin mustache a quick brushing. "I don't get the connection."

"Grants and sponsorships take time. In the short term, in order to stay open we need donations of any amount. If the public hears someone at Yates Health didn't handle matters correctly with a mentally challenged person, it will cause people who'd otherwise donate to stay away. Mystery Woman is becoming a folk hero."

Wills drummed the pen, one-two, on his notebook page. "Okay. I understand." Wills looked around a room of metal filing cabinets and the metal desk. He seemed lost in thought. Then he said, "Did she mention any family members? Or friends? Someone she'd recently been with?"

I told myself to stay still.

"She didn't mention anyone." Another lie. Edwina had mentioned Luther Burbank a few times. "She seemed completely alone."

"Did you tell anyone else what you've told me?"

"Inez Vasquez, my supervisor. I told her last night. After Mystery Woman was killed. I was shaken up, just driving around, and dropped by Inez's house to talk."

Wills thanked me for my time. He asked if I'd come in to talk again if requested.

"I'll help in any way I can."

Wills stood. He led me to the door and opened it. At shaking hands, Wills held on longer than was normal. "Dr. Taylor," he said, "I think you're hiding something."

"Because I'm nervous, talking about how I may have screwed up?"

Wills let go. His fingers gave the mustache another quick going over. "You have yourself a good evening."

I'd not taken three steps down the barren hallway before hearing the door shut. A sense of foreboding swept over my shoulders. How anxious had I appeared?

Saturday's outing with Bianca was to Dillon Beach. It was her favorite because it was the only beach where dogs were allowed, and Inez would not go further with household pets than the lone goldfish in Bianca's bedroom. We kicked her red bouncy ball back and forth before eating. After downing more food than you'd imagine a nine-year-old could, Bianca asked a woman, who was flinging a tennis ball with a handheld device, if she could try. The woman's throws sent her large Dalmatian charging into foamy surf to retrieve the ball.

"It's called a Chuck-it," the woman said. "Come on, I'll show you how."

The woman and Bianca looked to me to see if it was okay.

"Go for it."

Life was settling down. Everything around me may have been nothing more than an endless dream, but relaxed, on a blanket on sand, the breeze fresh, people enjoying whatever life is, was beginning to feel good again.

I read *Wild Oats in Eden*, a book about Sonoma County in the nineteenth century, until hearing Bianca shout, "Thank you!" She ran to our blanket and jammed a hand into a brown grocery bag holding peanut butter cookies.

"That dog is so cool!"

"Yeah. I saw."

On the drive to Appleton, Bianca, secure under a seatbelt in back, fell asleep. Once home she woke up and ran inside to tell Inez about flinging the soaked tennis ball into the ocean and the dog retrieving it. Before Inez had a chance to brew a pot of tea, I slapped five with Bianca and said I'd see her next Saturday. Inez gave me a probing look. She didn't ask where I was going. That was our way.

I drove to SunSpot, and took a roundabout route to the blue tarp. Once inside the hollowed-out redwood trunk, on blankets, eyes closed, a peacefulness enveloped me. It was warm in there, like a womb.

Eighteen

For a week, Mystery Woman stories topped the front section of the *Daily Democrat*. With no solid information coming forth—my interview with Lieutenant Wills was not mentioned—Edwina's heroic action faded from the mainstream press. An online group formed to try to identify the victim, and driver. Its participants had nothing to work from other than speculations and unfounded conspiracy theories.

On Monday, during my half-hour lunch break, I walked down Main Street to Yates General. Kurt Sanderson was at the desk between the groceries and artsy sections. Reading some kind of list, he made pencil checks as he went. Brown-framed glasses sat on his nose. The stretchy black band attached to them draped onto both shoulders. I was only a few feet away when Sanderson looked up. He let the glasses fall from his sunburned nose.

"I was wondering when you'd come by. Or if you would."

"Is there somewhere we can talk?"

"Let's go out back."

We passed through the arts and crafts section of the store. Adjacent to a bookshelf that contained works by local authors, was a door. Sanderson unlocked it. "This is our version of a break room," he said.

Behind the store was a deck. Two small round tables, two chairs at each. Past these were two Adirondack chairs painted blue. Sanderson sat in one, I the other. A small table had dust-covered magazines on top held down by painted-white stones. Sanderson folded his hands behind his head and waited for me to speak.

"Did you go to the police about me asking questions about Mystery Woman?"

Sanderson looked toward redwood trees that covered the neighboring hillside. A breeze carried their fresh scent. "I did not. I didn't want to needlessly get you involved, when I'm sure you did nothing wrong. Have you talked to them?"

"I went into Santa Rosa the day after. I told them what I told you, plus a few more details. I didn't mention our conversation." I joined Sanderson in looking uphill into forest. "I appreciate you keeping our conversation private, because I want to follow any leads that might bring me to the person who ran over her. If the police start questioning me about our conversation, or checking up on me, it will make things more difficult."

Sanderson's appearance reminded me of a group of senior citizen surfers I'd seen a few times at Salmon Creek Beach when jogging there. Decades of sun and salt water gave their skin a semi-shiny golden patina.

He said, "I'm glad you came by. I'd like to explain something to you, about West County. Separate from the horrible accident. You know, because you're still fairly new around here."

"Okay."

Sanderson unclasped his hands and wrapped them over edges of the Adirondack chair's wide armrests. "There's a particular ecosystem to West County. It's rich and varied, but in some ways it's fragile."

"It's the most livable place I've ever been," I said.

Sanderson grinned, bringing light to his cheeks. "Exactly. And beneath the surface of it are all kinds of moving parts. They don't always work in unison, yet they do work together."

"That's pretty vague."

He took a slow breath. "You're right. Let me try it this way. Sometimes there are things that can't be changed. They're in the past. So it's better to, you know, sit back and enjoy the universe."

"Why don't you want me to look into the death of an innocent person?"

A bigger grin this time. And a mini chuckle, to himself and not me. "Mystery Woman, who nobody knows anything about, is gone. No one can bring her back. Let me ask you a question. Is it possible prying into matters could have a negative effect on the West County ecosystem? With no long-term gains for the region?"

"Let me ask you a question. Do you know Alex Moran?"

Sanderson used his upper teeth to scratch his lower lip. He seemed to be deciding how to answer my question. "Not socially, but yes, I know him. When the great recession hit in 2008, city folks largely quit coming out here and watering our local economy. By 2010, a third of the businesses in town had closed, and others were going broke. That included Yates General. Mr. Moran, new here at the time, heard how bad things were and lent me money until things turned around. He's the reason

Yates still has a grocery store, a place where everyone in the community crosses paths."

"Same thing with Covid?"

"No. I took a business loan from the Feds. Why are you interested in Mr. Moran?"

"I met him in circumstances I can't describe. Let's call it doctor-patient confidentially. He's a little off."

"You said the same thing about Mystery Woman."

"You know, I guess I did. Maybe I'm too negative."

Sanderson stood. "Could you stay here a minute?"

Sanderson re-entered Yates General. Seconds later he came out holding Edwina's remaining drawing, half a dozen California golden poppies with no background other than green shading. Staying on his feet, Sanderson handed me the drawing.

"A belated welcome-to-town gift. On me. The work you folks do at the clinic is vital to that ecosystem I didn't describe very well."

"I can't take it."

"You two had some kind of friendship. She was paid for the drawing when she brought it in. Really, you should have it."

Seated in the low Adirondack chair, I reached to hand the drawing back. Sanderson strode to the door. He opened it.

"You can walk behind the building on your way to Yates Health."

Sanderson went inside and locked the door.

Feeling strange, but in truth wanting the poppies drawing, I put it in the Subaru. Inside Yates Health, Robin handed me a Post-it with a phone number written on it. "Mayor Carbone called. You know who he is?"

"Yes."

"He says he has some news."

"Great." Illogically, I thought the news might be information regarding Edwina.

With ten minutes before my next appointment, I went to my examining room and called Carbone. His voice stirred more gravel than I remembered, and was delivered in what I thought of as a California Country Twang. After pleasantries, Carbone got down to business.

"It looks like Hollywood is coming to West County." Carbone did not sound thrilled. "Usually, it's car commercials. This is a movie. Not big time, not penny ante. The film commission put the people making it in contact with me. They need someone to help with scouting places to shoot. I recommended you."

"Why? You know West County better than anyone."

"That I do." I wondered if Carbone had a toothpick in his mouth and was scraping his teeth with it. "I don't much cotton to L.A. people," he said. "They're from a different planet. But to your question, they'll have to pay $200 an hour for your time. When I oversee traffic on car commercials, the money goes to the county general fund. With you, it can go to the clinic. I already cleared it with the powers that be. See where I'm coming from?"

"I like where you're coming from."

"Good. Write down this number." Carbone gave me a phone number with a 310 area code. "Chris Runnel. He's the director. Says he wrote the thing, too. Within reason, go along with whatever he says. If this works out, it could turn into decent money for Yates Health."

I thanked Carbone. And didn't believe his reason for choosing me to be liaison with the movie people. Even if his motive was one hundred percent to help Yates Health stay open, everyone else at the clinic had been in Sonoma County years longer than I had. Carbone had to have a motive.

"They say there'll be a car chase or two," Carbone said. "I suggest you use Ridge Road, the same stretch as in the commercials. I thought that area may be of interest to you. Give me your email."

Online searches had revealed Alex Moran lived on Ridge Road. I didn't ask what prompted Carbone's comment about me possibly having an interest in the area. My number one priority was keeping Yates Health afloat.

"What's the movie about?"

"Hell if I know. Call him and find out."

Sandy, a better candidate for the assignment because of her frequent rural bike rides, passed by as I walked to Inez's office at the end of the hall. The door was open. Eyes on the screen to her left, she typed intently. Inez's thick hair was held in a pink-orange hair tie, the kind often worn on a woman's wrist. The room smelled of jasmine tea. A ceramic cup I recognized from Inez's house was to her right.

"Do you have a minute?" I asked.

"I have one minute."

"I've been on the phone with Mayor Carbone."

"Trouble with one of ours?" Inez meant one of our patients.

"We have a chance to raise some money. How much I can't guess."

Inez quit typing. "I just got another minute."

I scooted a wood chair to near Inez's desk. "Carbone's an intriguing guy. How well do you know him?"

"He contacts me when someone in far county is having a health crisis, or if he suspects domestic violence. In that case he'll want to know if it's a patient, and if we've had suspicions. I contact him for the same type of stuff. Something I think he should know." Inez squinched her eyes together, rubbed them with thumbs and forefingers. "You mentioned the word money."

I relayed the conversation with Carbone.

"Frank wouldn't have called if it wasn't solid."

"Why do you think he chose me? We don't even know each other."

"You driving all over to help people who can't get to town. That kind of thing is big in Frank's book. I guarantee you he's heard about it." Inez placed her hands on the keyboard; she was ready to get back to work. "He pretty much knows everyone living off the beaten path."

"How about if I come over for dinner? Let's celebrate."

Inez made a huffing sound. "You're trying to get me to go home on time. To not ask Linda if Bianca can stay late. I'm onto you, Taylor." Inez reached across the desk. We squeezed each other's hand. She said, "We'd love to have you over tonight."

"What should I bring?"

"Only yourself. Oh, and no more wall ball. I can't get all the chalk marks out. Redwood's too porous."

"Sorry."

"I don't think so. You've been having too much fun to be sorry."

Nineteen

Chris Runnel, the movie director I phoned after Carbone called, spoke in sentences of few words. While researching him I was surprised to learn he was sixty-one years old. He sounded much younger. He had short gray hair advancing to white, a bluntly-trimmed snowy beard. Along with his voice sounding younger than his age, the cast and themes of his movies were most often youth-centered. Runnel said he and his assistant, Dale, would fly to Santa Rosa the next Thursday to check out West County for two days. Runnel asked if there was an Olympic-sized pool available for his morning swim.

"I start my days after an hour in the water," he said.

Remembering Carbone's advice about giving L.A. people what they want in exchange for their money, I said, "I'll find one."

"Terrific. Dale will take things from here until we're up north. You're like what, a couple hours from Oregon?"

"A couple of hundred miles plus."

"Really? I'll have to look at a map. I rarely get north of Ventura. Dale pitched your area for shooting. Knows it from kid camps."

Sandy and Storm agreed to cover for me when the movie people visited; the ambulance ride had lessened friction between Storm and myself. I emailed a contract to Runnel, taken from one emailed to me by Carbone, with Yates Health inserted in the places County of Sonoma had been in the original. The message and contract were CC'd to Inez.

On the appointed day, at shortly past noon, Runnel, his assistant and I met outside a newish motel on Highway 116 south of downtown Appleton. They'd taken an Uber from the airport and checked in. Chris Runnel looked like he did online—fit, self-controlled. He wore well-traveled maroon cords, a green flannel shirt that reminded me of campouts, and scuffed hiking boots.

Dale turned out to be Dalinda Hayes, early thirties, slim, hair dyed whitish blonde with a two-inch purple stripe running from a center part down over her left ear. She exuded a cool hipness accompanied by an aura of crisp competence. Dale's toned frame was tucked into unwrinkled skinny jeans. Her thin gold sweater and dark running shoes looked fresh out of a box.

Neither showed the least surprise at shaking my half hand. Their eyes did meet at seeing my rusty brown Subaru Outback, their limo for the next two days.

"Cool," Runnel said. He got in the passenger seat.

Dale toted a mushroom colored canvas bag, which she positioned on the bench seat in back when climbing in. "No promises," she said. "We have another possibility."

"Understood." The engine came to life. "I'll start macro, to give you a taste of the area. Assuming that's okay with you. From there, give me specific needs."

"Sounds good," Runnel said. Looking ahead, he stroked his clipped short snowy beard.

We headed west. Sun streamed through the windows. Outside Appleton, oak trees, then a vineyard. Tiny flowers, orange, pinkish, some yellow, some purple, made for a tapestry hillside. We bounced along without talking. Runnel seemed to click mental photographs of everything we passed. Dale kept her phone perched, as if atop an invisible desk. She recorded Runnel's observations.

We didn't stop in Yates. We climbed through redwoods and out Duncan's Valley. I was doing my best to show off the grandness of the region. Shadows hovered under thickly woven branches. Drivers passing from the other direction waved hellos. We reached the ridge near SunSpot. West, far off, lines of clouds were striped, silvery, gray, the faintest of blues. At the horizon it was not possible to distinguish sky from sea.

"I don't know anything about making a movie," I said, "but these views would look great on a big screen. The ocean from way up here. Point Reyes. Looking into the mouth of Tomales Bay."

Dale pressed forward. Her whitish-blonde hair and purple stripe showed between the two front seats. "Chris. Think *Falling Home*." *Falling Home* was the title of Runnel's most successful movie at the box office. "Those shots in the mountains with the soundtrack playing? Remember how quiet the audience always got? Shoot here when Kiya's alone, driving aimlessly, sure she'll never get Doug to love her. You'll break people's hearts."

Runnel said, "Yep."

To me, Dale said, "Kiya's the name of our lead. She's a sixteen-year-old who gets addicted to stealing cars."

We dropped to the ocean, drove north. To our left waves smashed rocks. We crossed the Russian River and proceeded to Bishop's Grade, which took us inland to Ridge Road. To both sides were old low fences of thin redwood slats. Their gray surfaces were dotted with spots of orange lichen.

I watched addresses that were posted roadside. The parcels were large. Few houses were in view. At Moran's address, number 4600, a dirty yellow school bus waited for us to pass. I looked straight ahead, then in the rear-view mirror saw the bus slowly turn onto pavement.

I drove faster than normal and took the first opportunity to head down to the coast highway. We stopped at tiny Ocean Cove Store for deviled egg sandwiches on white bread chock full of mayonnaise. Runnel and Dale seemed tickled at the fatty, home-made fare, as if it were an exotic binge compared to their meals in Los Angeles. We ate while sitting in the car.

Runnel pointed across the roadway to the shack-like store. "Dale?"

"I'm on it."

Dale went outside and clicked pictures of the store, which was one room about the size of the living room in an ample suburban house. She climbed back in. Dale and Runnel discussed a sequence of scenes in the planned movie.

What was Rick Fulton doing at Moran's? They were not two people I could imagine being friends. I wondered how Kim's hand was coming along, yet wondered more about the yellow bus exiting the road leading to Moran's place, which according to Zillow was two thousand square feet plus outbuildings on eighty-seven acres.

Runnel said. "This is like a vacation. What else can you present?"

"Do you like seals?"

"Love seals."

"He actually does," Dale said, popping forward again.

"I'll show you seals in Jenner. You catch one's eye, sometimes it'll follow when you walk down the beach."

And so the afternoon sailed along, with me showing Runnel and Dale everything I could think of before taking them to their hotel in Appleton.

We got out.

"List," Runnel said.

Dale reached into her canvas bag and pulled out a manila envelope. She opened it and slipped out two printed pages stapled together. Dale handed them to me. "For your eyes only."

"Those are locations we need to shoot," Runnel said. "Tomorrow, show us places you think can work for them."

"Got it. What time?"

"I thought you said open swimming begins at eight, at a public pool in town."

"I'll be in the lobby at seven-thirty. Get you back for breakfast by nine-thirty."

"I never eat breakfast," Runnel said.

Dale said, "That's how he keeps his figure."

They started for the hotel entrance.

"Will you be swimming?"

Dale flipped the purple stripe of hair; it looked like wind blew it sideways. "I'll be doing push-ups."

That night I made notes on the locations pages, which listed things such as *middle-class neighborhood; house for teen party;*

teen eating hangout; two country roads; high school; part-time job place for Kiya; four believable sites to steal a car. And the like. I wrote in streets and buildings that seemed right, getting addresses online, using Google Maps to check my memory, and noting details about places that stood out in my mind.

Friday morning, post Runnel's swim in the pool at Forester Park, the three of us started the location scouting with Appleton residential streets. Inez's street was avoided so there couldn't later be claims of favoritism. Next we looked at commercial establishments with Runnel talking in movie-lingo and Dale recording his words. He spoke in brief, cogent paragraphs. After a late lunch I took them to the small town of Forestville. The original high school had been turned into a continuation school campus, Laguna, with a smallish student body. It had empty hallways and unused classrooms suited for scenes taking place at school. Dale shot photos, as did Runnel. I delivered them to the airport in time for a five-thirty-five flight to LAX, carrying their bags, thinking about the money to come in from Runnel's movie.

Runnel shook my hand. "Listen, if we shoot here, the guild will demand a doctor on set when an under-eighteen drives at night, even though she won't be going fast. Also for two fake car chases. Later we'll speed them up to music."

"Maybe for the fight scene," Dale said, "with Doug and the bad guy. One of them will probably be under eighteen."

Runnel nodded, turned to me. "Would you be available?"

"I'll help in any way I can."

Twenty

With no Saturday open gym, I took Bianca and Ellen to the Snoopy Ice Arena in Santa Rosa. They'd both ice skated a few times and enjoyed gliding past my clumsy first efforts at circling the rink. Midafternoon was a schoolmate's birthday party. Inez took the girls to that.

I headed north. My phone jingled. On its face: Carbone. I pulled into the lot at Andy's Produce. Cars whizzed by on Highway 116.

"How did it go with the L.A. people?" Unlike Chris Runnel, the sound of Carbone's voice matched his age.

"They say they're also considering someplace else, but I could tell they fell in love with it here. They say they'll need a doctor on site whenever their lead actress drives at night. Maybe for a few more scenes."

"Cha-ching," Carbone said.

"By the way," I said, "I'm wondering if you know someone. My understanding is he lives off the grid in northwest county."

"You name him, I'll know him."

"Rick Fulton."

Carbone breathed, out and audibly in again. "A troubled

heart. Rick's got demons picked up in the second Iraq. What about him?"

"When I was showing the movie people around, on Ridge Road in fact, I saw him at the wheel of this old school bus."

"Whereabouts on Ridge?"

"An address marker said forty-six hundred."

"That's a man named Alex Moran's place."

The line went quiet. I didn't know what I could say without revealing more than I wanted.

Finally, I said, "A while back I took Fulton's partner, a woman named Kim Johnson, in an ambulance to Santa Rosa. She and Fulton showed up in Yates in the bus, stoned to the gills. She'd cut off half of two fingers. Fulton rode in the ambulance with me. He was… intense, highly agitated on top of the pot. Also kind of interesting."

"Of course I know Rick and Kim. Also know about her hand. You could have checked in with me on that. When we met at the accident site."

"I had no idea you knew them."

"I know them. Rick's a good handyman. Lots of people hire him out here. Everything from roofs to plumbing. Nothing electrical. Electricity freaks him out. Tied to his war scars."

"I understand. We talked about it."

"Listen, my wife's sister and her husband will be here any minute. I just wanted to see how things went. So you showed 'em where I think a car chase could best be filmed? Right along there at 4600?"

"They loved it," I lied. If I had mentioned the area for car chases, Runnel would have said to stop. Rick Fulton would likely have seen me and wondered what I was up to.

We said goodbyes. I didn't remember seeing any carpentry tools during my brief time inside the smelly school bus. I did remember the wet suit, mask, snorkel, fins and a spear gun haphazardly piled in a corner. I remembered the abalone in the Styrofoam ice chests I delivered. The sea turtles, too.

I continued north, crossing the Russian River as on Thursday. Twisty miles of climbing hilly terrain, curves followed by curves. A mix of forest and grasslands. My destination, a place new to me, was Wathor Mountain. You went up Bishop's Grade to Ridge Road, then to Wathor Mountain Road. Power lines ended at Wathor Mountain Road.

County tax records showed a sixty-acre parcel owned by a Kimberly Johnson. The road was unpredictable. The going became cumbersome. I came to a gated dirt road, on the left. No address marker. A sheet of weathered plywood leaned horizontally against a nearby oak tree. Painted on it, in black:

UNDER THIS TREE IS

THE LAST MAN TO TRESPASS

The sagging gate was comprised of lashed together, once-white plastic pipes. A line of curling razor wire was suspended above its top. The crude fence was secured to a log post by a wrapped chain and a heavy lock. To both sides of the gate ran barbed wire fences six feet high. I parked in front of the gate, and broke a peaceful silence by honking the horn, three slow calls, then reached to the backseat for my doctor's bag. I stood in front of the car with my hands visible. It was quite possible nobody was around to hear the horn.

The peaceful silence, which had re-settled over everything, was broken by the sound of shifting engine gears. The yellow bus came into view. Its engine sounded like a slow-moving locomotive in that otherwise muted wilderness. The bus made half a circle over grass and halted when perpendicular to the makeshift gate. The folding door opened. Rick Fulton stepped out. He wiped a hand across a forehead glistening with sweat. He hadn't shaved in days.

Surprised to see me out there, Rick said, "What the hell?"

He wore cutoff jeans with white strings unraveling from where the jeans had been trimmed and left rough. Unlike the rest of his face, the meandering purple scar was bone dry. No sweat. Rick didn't smile and he didn't walk to the gate.

"I'm here to check on Kim. Dr. Wun's office says she skipped her appointment. No phone call or email explanation. Did you get their messages?"

A frown, followed by a shaking head. "It's two hours to get there. A round trips costs like fifty bucks in gas for this thing. So she's doing what they said from here. Better than driving into the world and letting their machines mess with her head."

"Really, someone needs to take a look."

"I been keeping it clean, watching for infection. Helped dudes in the desert when no medics showed. She's—"

The creaking sound of the bus's folding door stopped Rick's words. Kim stepped down, waving a small cast that encircled the two re-attached fingers. She smiled shyly.

"Hello. How are you?" I asked.

In just two weeks Kim was noticeably changed. Her frizzy blonde hair was trained into twin ponytails. Her top and jeans looked freshly laundered. The biggest change was her face. Kim was clear eyed. Her cheeks held a dash of color, and she looked well-rested. "I finally got straight," she said. "No pot, no alcohol, no sugar." Kim gave the mini cast another wave. "I figure it'll help with this."

"It'll help with everything," I said.

"Me, too. Kind of," Rick said. "I still like my red wine. And a puff here and there."

Kim gave Rick a mischievous gaze. "Don't you mean you're in love with red wine?"

"I admit to a crush on Madame Cabernet."

"Aren't you going to invite our guest in?"

Rick reached into a pocket of the ragged cutoffs, extracted a lone key. He unlocked the gate. Once freed from the log post, the gate of old pipes dragged the ground. I set my doctor's bag aside and helped open it.

Rick disappeared inside the bus.

Kim looked at me. "They said the fingers only have a chance because you didn't wait for a helicopter."

Rick stepped out of the bus holding three folding chairs. He placed them in a triangle and tested them for stability. We sat. Rick watched closely as I removed the slip cast from Kim's re-attached fingers. She moaned in discomfort. Rick held her left hand. I asked her to try to move the fingers, swollen to almost double normal size and encircled in stitches thicker than the fulsome ones I'd used to draw Odin's wound tight. With effort Kim moved her fingers an eighth of an inch up, about the same down.

"Painful?"

"More incredibly stiff than painful. It's like I got hundred-year-old fingers. They put screws in to attach the bones. That's where there's pain."

"Try to open them all the way."

Kim couldn't straighten out her fingers.

"It'll come," I said. "Try a few times every day. Stop if it hurts too much."

"She's doing good," Rick said.

Kim said to me, "What do you think?"

"I don't know anything about it, except to say don't push things. Think more in terms of a year than weeks or months."

We were quiet in that silent land. I gently washed the fingers with antiseptic. Rick kept up his close watch.

"It'll be a while longer," I said, "but these stitches are going to have to come out."

Kim said, "You can do that, right?"

"Don't let anybody work on your hand except Dr. Wun. When he tells me he thinks it's time, I'll let you folks know. I'm happy to drive you, round trip. Save you gas money."

I dipped fresh Q-tips in the antiseptic, moved them in circles against the inner wall of the slip cast.

"I'll do that next time," Rick said.

I finished and closed the doctor's bag. Rick went inside the bus. He came out with a plastic jug of water and three canning jars. He poured.

"Coming here reminds me of someone I recently met," I said. "He lives down on Ridge Road. I'm told he does a lot for the locals. You folks kind of got your own ecosystem going out here."

Rick tossed down water. He looked to Kim with evident warmth. I wondered how often she still noticed the horrific purple scar that curved down his face and neck. I hoped rarely.

"Our neighbors, we're each others' peeps," Rick said.

I remembered the brief meeting with the Finnegans at the hospital. What did these isolated people do every day? "Do you folks know a guy named Alex Moran? That's who I met."

Rick looked up, frowned. His eyebrows pulled closer together. He ran a hand through his wild long brown hair. If I hadn't seen the bus leave Moran's property, I would have believed Rick when he said, "Heard of him. Never actually met him."

"Me, either," Kim said. "I know he's helped a lot of people. Everyone says he made a pile in tech and quit the whole scene. At like twenty-nine. Very cool."

"That's what I heard," I said, though Kim's words were news to me. "I should go. Stay hydrated. Walk every day. Keep your stamina up even though you can't use the hand."

Kim said she'd do that.

"You're going to get through this, Love," Rick said. "Know it."

I collected my doctor's bag. "Let me help with the gate."

On the way down Wathor Mountain, it clicked: The phrase *Know it* came from gatherings, referred to as The Sessions, Shannon had mentioned took place at Moran's. I'd found comments about them, though only half a dozen, online when researching him. There was a bare bones, black and white website. The home page stated Stay Tuned. No quotes, no testimonials. Below Stay Tuned was listed a next The Sessions gathering. These were afternoon congregations Moran held and charged attendees $350 dollars for. No regular schedule could be found. From comments online The Sessions seemed a mixture of New Age thinking, something called postural integration, and chanting affirmations. Apparently, The Sessions shepherded you to a state wherein you *Know it*. What that was remained, at least to me, undefined.

Twenty-one

Odin didn't make an appearance when I picked up the van at dawn on Sunday; I was glad to be done with him. The route had become routine, and when my heart ticked up at seeing another vehicle or anything slightly out of place, I whispered a mantra: "Last time. Last time. Last time."

Sunday dinner was the usual at Homer's, with an exception being I asked Kendra if we could speak for a minute in the kitchen area. She remembered me leaving abruptly that night. When I told her about being drugged, after expressing shock, Kendra said she hadn't noticed anything suspicious.

"On weekends, customers are about half people from out of town. There's always some you don't know."

The work week that followed was upbeat because Yates Health was getting a steady stream of donations. Besides the thousand-dollar check from Moran, and the twenty-four hundred dollars to come from Runnel's production company, dozens of contributions, a few not modest, were coming in as a result of the *Daily Democrat's* article about the plight of the clinic.

The next Saturday morning began the every-six-weeks overnight Bianca spent at her dad's, who she never mentioned to me. Inez would drive Bianca an hour and a half to Willets, return home and replicate the trip on Sunday afternoon. While Inez drove Bianca, I packed a lunch and bottled water, and drove to SunSpot. Edwina's hollowed redwood tree trunk had become a refuge, a place to relax and think about things. I ate and napped on the tan blankets. I'd left them neatly flat and they, like everything else in there, remained untouched. What kept animals away I chalked up to Edwina's spirit, sensed instinctively such that creatures didn't tear off the tarp.

After hiking uphill to where the land flattened, I proceeded up the dirt road to my car. Slotted next to it was a Sonoma County Sheriff's Department cruiser. The driver's window was open. In uniform, behind the wheel, reading a paperback book, sat Mayor Carbone. He threw me a gray smile.

"What brings you here?" I asked, assuming the answer was me.

"In-laws left yesterday. I've been negligent on making rounds. Even took three days off in a row. How about we have ourselves a confab?"

Carbone got out of the patrol car, hitched his slacks and rested his back side against the left front fender. He squinted. "I was thinking the same thing. What brings you here?"

Without me seeing where it came from, Carbone had a toothpick out and scraped it between teeth. This caused his mouth to open and his wrinkles to shift and deepen. A voice on the car radio crackled. It rattled off two street names followed by law code numbers. Carbone tipped his head toward the open window.

I motioned toward land and sea. "This is my go-to spot. I take a hike, then drive to the beach and run. I'm determined to get back in good shape."

Carbone nodded, scraped his teeth. "Enter my name in an internet search, you get nothing but my job, and my salary comes up as public record. Type your name in, you hit a jackpot. Basketball star. Doctor. Articles about the work accident that screwed up your hand. Articles about your heroism. All that," Carbone said, "is laudable. One thing though." Carbone waved a forefinger in the air. "I have to say, over the past dozen years a handful of people in your orbit have ended up deceased."

He shook his head and looked troubled.

"If you've read about me, you know I was a private snoop for a lot of that time. My childhood friend Brett Boyd? I was the one who caught his murderer."

Carbone slipped the toothpick in a shirt pocket of his uniform. He looked off. His grayness of face and sideburns reminded me of a venerable great blue heron. And like the old birds, Carbone had become stick thin. He grimaced. "It's just that there's a pattern. You meet Mystery Woman after she helps out Inez's daughter, when the kid got lost. You meet Mystery Woman here a few times. She ends up deceased."

"What's this really about?"

"Before coming here, I went to Yates General. Had a conversation with Kurt Sanderson. He says you knew Mystery Woman."

"I've never hidden it. I went into Santa Rosa the day after she was hit, and made a statement to a Lieutenant Wills."

"He told me what you said. That how I know you knew her."

"Wills told me it was between the two of us."

"That means between you and the police, not the public." Carbone fished out his toothpick, whittled his gray teeth. "Here's the thing. Kurt says you're more than a little interested in the young woman's death. Says you're obsessed with finding who was responsible. Like you want to take matters into your own hands."

I stepped back, bumping against the passenger door of my car and faintly rocking it. "I'm going to find who hit her, and drag his ass in."

Carbone took me by the elbow. With his other hand he removed the toothpick from his mouth. "Here in West County we're kind of live and let live. Peace and prosperity fare better by not being too particular about things."

Readying myself for another description of the area's unique human ecosystem, I looked into Carbone's gray face. "I think I know what you mean."

"Live and let live. At the same time, if the let live part gets dropped, I got to get particular. Restore things to a healthy balance. At the moment, my region strikes me as out of balance. It'll take some time, but I plan to fix that."

"Could you be more specific?"

Carbone straightened his frame. He let go of my elbow. "No. For now, I'm instructing you to fill me in on anything you think you learn about Mystery Woman's death. This is between you, me, and that pretty blue sky up there."

"Lieutenant Wills?"

Carbone's gaze intensified. "I've made myself clear enough. You and I want the same thing. Because of the people potentially involved, I have to be a little quiet about it—don't ask for names. Keep me in the loop, and I won't ask you about a redwood tree trunk made into a little house."

My head seemed to fill with steam. It affected my hearing, and balance on the sloped dirt road. I couldn't launch a reply.

Carbone said, "I think that's a fair exchange."

More steam rose within. With vision as well as balance off, I walked around the front of the Subaru to the driver's door, got in and drove away. Though he talked in a roundabout way, Carbone had made it clear he wanted Edwina's killer caught. My guess was he wanted more than that. I guessed Carbone had decided things had gotten out of hand in his domain, and that among other things, Moran's operation had to go.

Twenty-two

I grew more attentive to life at Yates Health, contributing ideas at meetings, regularly taking evening appointments with people who couldn't afford to miss work. Wednesday dinners at Inez's house became the norm. Wall ball games were replaced with tutoring Bianca on her elementary school's basketball court that had hoops at eight feet high rather than the standard ten.

Home, on the couch typing an email response to a patient's query about her medications, my phone jingled. No name showed. I answered with a hello.

"Doctor Taylor?"

A woman's voice, youngish.

"Everyone calls me Jeff. This is?"

"Kendra Monroe, from Homer's."

"Thanks for calling." I pictured Kendra, brown hair tucked under a red San Francisco Forty-Niners baseball cap. Freckles. Her warm smile. "How can I help you?"

"It hit me today," she said. "There was something different that night. This couple comes in about once a month. They stick out because they always make comments like, 'Wow, electric lights and everything.' They let you know they live off the grid. They kind of show off about it."

My pulse ticked up. "Did the guy have a major scar on his face and neck? You wouldn't miss it."

"No. Why?"

"Someone came to mind." I grabbed a pen, turned over an opened envelope, and scored lines. "What about them?"

"They come into town to stock up. Like I said, about once a month."

"What do they look like? How old do you think they are?"

"Forty. No. More like thirties with high miles. Skinny. She calls him Jimbo. I have no idea what her name is. Coming in on a Sunday night, instead of on a shopping day, it was a first. They acted a little weirder than normal. I figured they were high. They've come in high before."

"Did they leave shortly after me?"

"I don't think so. I can't say for sure."

"Do you know what they drive?"

"Sorry. That's another no. Can you promise not to tell anyone about this call?"

"No problem. Do you have reason to be afraid of them?"

"They give off a weird vibe. I don't want them to know we talked."

"It's a promise."

We exchanged goodbyes. I walked little circles in the house without halls. The Finnegans, close friends of Kim and Rick, living a mile down Wathor Mountain Road from them. Did Odin, out of revenge, pay or otherwise get them to drug me? If so, how did Odin know them? I was thinking Rick Fulton for the abalone and turtles because of the gear in the bus. Maybe the salmon. Kim wasn't out of the question as far as those went. Jim and Joan for the venison and quail? If so, that meant he or they had a rifle. Poaching salmon meant owning or having access to a sea-worthy motorboat.

Although life hadn't completely returned to normal, I was letting go of questions caused by the drug trip and largely not trying to figure out the mysteries of existence. The days rolled into late May. Hillside grasses turned brown.

I left work at noon on a Friday. I made a house call in hills outside the town of Monte Rio. The patient was on oxygen, had extreme edema and trouble getting around. From there, acting as a middleman man between Dr. Wun, and Kim and Rick, I set out for Wathor Mountain. Driving Ridge Road north, well before reaching the 4600-address marking pole, I came upon a woman wearing a yellow safety vest. Carrying a Hefty bag, she was picking up litter. I parked on a dirt spot, got out and strolled toward her, wondering if she were related to activities at Moran's compound. The woman watched me approach. Her jeans and tennis shoes showed dust. Her hair was under a dark knit cap that protected her head from an insistent spring wind. Crinkling her eyes, she looked at me with suspicion.

I attempted to put her at ease. "Hello. I'm Doctor Taylor, from the Yates Health clinic. I'm making a house call and need some help with directions."

She bent at the knees, set the olive-colored Hefty bag roadside. "Where are you trying to get to?"

"Wathor Mountain Road."

The woman, whose name turned out to be Miley, gave directions. She asked if I needed to write it down.

"Got it," I said. "I'm curious. Do you work for the county?"

Miley laughed. "Retired from UPS. Bought a cabin where Ridge Road meets Wathor. Once a week I pick up litter till the legs give out. Begin where I left off last time, till I reach the end of Ridge. Then start over. Takes a few months to cover it all." Miley's eyes shined the light of a feisty soul. "God's country is too grand a blessing to let trash stain it like they do."

"They?"

"Mainly tourists. Who you looking for on Wathor?"

"The patient's name is Kim Johnson. She lives with a fellow named Rick Fulton."

Miley's good cheer vanished. "I guess you have to help everybody." She looked up and around, perhaps remembering she was standing in God's country. "Ah. Don't listen to a lonely old lady. They just rub me the wrong way. Barrel past my place in an old school bus like they're in a race. Wakes me every time if it's night."

"Sorry to hear it."

Moran's Escalade hummed past, sounding quieter than you'd think, considering its weight. It pulled over after passing my Subaru. One of the huge tough guys climbed out, went around the front of the vehicle and opened the door for Moran. Soon as he came into view, Miley cringed.

"What in the world could *he* want?"

Moran walked toward us.

"You don't sound like you have a high opinion of him."

"He attracts too many weirdos. They go to his place for

séances. I hear orgies, too. Half of them spend the night camped out anywhere they please, playing music at all hours. I don't call the police because they can see my lights. They'd know who reported them."

Moran, in all black, came with his bodyguard staying a dozen paces behind him.

Miley scooped up the Hefty bag and crossed the road. She plucked an empty Budweiser can from grass. The wind hummed a high note. The sky was a soft looking pale blue.

Arriving, Moran put both hands in his pockets, surely so he wouldn't have to shake. He channeled a smile so taut it revealed no teeth. "What a coincidence." he said. "You crossed the mind about an hour ago, and here you are. Know it."

"Know what?"

"Know what you already know. Know your truth." The green marble swami eyes seemed to penetrate me like ex rays. Moran smoothly demanded, "Why are you at my place of residence? This is my land. Both sides of the road."

I explained I was going to Kim Johnson and Rick Fulton's place, wasn't sure about the roads, had stopped and asked Miley for directions.

"I'm taking them to Santa Rosa, to have Kim's hand looked at. She had an—"

"I-am-aware."

Sam or Bam stood with legs apart, hands clasped behind him. The wind skewed his long black beard like a windsock. Miley glanced in his direction, and spit.

"So you know them?" I asked.

"Rick works for me. He is analogous to a part-time handyman

for the property."

Moran had a strange vocabulary. And I was tired of him staring at me like I was an eye chart. So, verbally speaking, I poked him. "Know it," I said loudly. "If you'll excuse me, I have to take a patient to see her surgeon."

I walked past Moran, the dusting of face powder and peaches smell.

"You're excused," he said.

I called out a goodbye to Miley. Head down, she gave a negligible wave. Passing Bam or Sam, I whispered, "Know it."

I drove off. In the rear-view mirror I saw that Moran hadn't moved. Neither had the enormous bodyguard. I wondered what Moran was thinking.

The trip with Kim and Rick was mostly silent except engine sounds and the sounds of tires rolling over asphalt. Rick had bathed and shaved. Kim hummed a tune that carried spiritual overtones. They were polite to the point of borderline docile. At the doctor's office, Kim asked if Rick and I could go in with her, to help ask questions. Dr. Wun was a gentleman in his sixties. He treated them respectfully. Rick didn't mention tracking devices. By the time we got back to their place, we were all tired from the day's travels. I helped Rick with the drooping gate. The school bus was parked on the other side.

Twenty-three

"You're different," Inez said.

It was still light out. On our right sides, my left arm curled around her waist, we came down from cresting our pleasure mountain. The bed's cracked headboard hadn't made dents in the wall. There was no worry that neighbors heard screams. I understood exactly what Inez meant.

She said, "You seem a lot closer, especially at the end."

During the previous month, for me our lovemaking had drifted from slamming my way into ecstatic journeys to pouring love from my body into Inez's.

"Aren't you going to say anything?" she asked.

I marveled at the wood grain in the redwood wall next to the bed, the clarity of its individual lines. "I thought we weren't supposed to talk right after sex."

"Come on, Jeff. Talk."

"I like every way we make love."

"You're impossible."

Inez took my hand in both of hers. She rubbed her back against my stomach. We were still, and silent. We seemed to drift, like the mattress was a raft in a large body of water.

Inez said, "Are you different because of Teacher Lady? Did she change you?"

"Do you ever get tired of being right?"

Inez reached behind her, squeezed my hip. "I wish I could've met her."

"Me, too."

I got up to pee. After washing sweat off my face, and returning to bed, Inez took the bathroom. She shut the door. Water ran in the sink. My phone rang. I picked it up, thinking I wouldn't answer. The name that showed changed that.

"Mayor Carbone," I said. "How are you?"

"Has Rick Fulton called?"

"No. Why?"

"He called me hours ago. He was all wound up. Said he had to talk right away. Said he had things to admit—his word, admit. I advised him to call a lawyer I know, a good one, Debra Morehouse. Gave Rick the number. Told him since me and Debra are friends, Rick needed to speak with someone at headquarters, not me."

Inez came to bed, saw I was on the phone, gave an air kiss and went down the hall to the living room.

"That doesn't answer the question of why you phoned me."

"When Rick called, he said the way you've helped him and Kim, it got him thinking. Said he wanted to do the right thing. But he doesn't show at the department, like he agreed to. He doesn't answer Morehouse's calls, or mine."

"Was Kim coming with him?"

"I don't think so. The way he said I, and never we, makes me think she wasn't coming. I didn't ask questions, because I didn't want to hear things and later be asked about them by the department."

"How can I help?"

"Try his number. Maybe he'll answer for you. Let me know."

After updating Inez—we'd talked about Kim and Rick quite a bit since they'd showed up at the clinic that wild day—I called Rick's number. No answer. Left a message to call me right away. I texted Carbone, relaying this.

Inez said, "Let's go. I'll grab a sweater."

It was our once-in-six-weeks chance to spend the whole night together. On those we never left the house.

"Go where?"

"I care about them, too. If Rick's not there, we talk to Kim. See what we can find out."

It was dark before we reached the coast. My phone sang its tune. Driving a country road in the dark, I slipped out my phone and handed it go Inez.

"Carbone again," she said.

I pulled into someone's driveway. Inez handed me the phone.

"Any news?"

No cars passed on the road.

"You should sit down." Carbone's voice was lower, more gravelly than usual. It carried little force.

"Oh, crap."

"About twenty minutes ago, I got the call. Bus was found a hundred feet down a ravine off Wathor Mountain Road. No seat belt. He took a header through the windshield."

Inez, hearing this, touched her cheek.

"Who discovered it?"

150

"Only reason it was found was, a couple out driving around pulled over to take pictures. I didn't recognize their names. You can look all the way to Cobb Mountain from there. They smelled something that didn't seem right. They went to take a look."

"Was Kim with him?"

"No. And she knows. I made two calls right away. Their neighbors, the Finnegans, and Kim's friend Nina Sudmeier. Nina says she'll stay there as long as needed."

"Inez and I are on our way to their place now."

Carbone's inhale sounded like little rocks popping. "I'm going to look at where it happened. Then go see Kim and make it official."

"Should we come? Kim and I have a good connection."

The line went silent. Then Carbone said, "She already has three people up there. Two more would be too many. That poor fellow," Carbone added, "could be a jerk. But he wasn't a bad jerk, if that makes any sense."

"It makes perfect sense. Rick had a big heart."

"Go on home. Watch out for crazy drivers on these roads at night."

Twenty-four

In bed holding each other, Inez and I didn't sleep much. Rick Fulton, army veteran, who we later learned had been awarded a bronze star for valor on the battlefield, was gone at forty-two. I remembered Rick impulsively hugging me in Memorial Hospital after sitting with him when Kim's fingers were being reattached. Remembered him carrying glass canning jars and pouring water. Remembered thinking that Kim's accident might help Rick turn his life around.

In the morning, Mayor Carbone called to say the authorities found a bottle of tranquilizers in the bus, and two empty beer bottles that weren't dry on the inside. "He was wound tight as a sprocket when he called. He talked so fast I had trouble following it. I'm not surprised he took something before heading in."

I thanked Carbone for the information, hung up and relayed what he'd said to Inez. "I don't like it. A guy like Rick, one of his tranquilizers, even two, and two beers are nothing. He wouldn't drive off a cliff."

"I get it. You didn't get a chance to save him." Inez gently rocked me, kept me close. "You couldn't save Mystery Woman, either. You think you're supposed to save everyone."

"Not now. Okay?"

Inez said, "At twenty-five you solved a case about a state senator. A few years later you ran down the two men who killed Karen's grandfather."

"Karen's grandfather was a saint."

"A saint, like Mystery Woman."

"Ine," I said, "if someone forced Rick off the road, I'm going to find him and bring him in. I'm going to find who killed Mystery Woman and do the same."

"Why can't you let go of anything?"

"Like I said, not now. I've got too much to think about."

"You are absolutely impossible."

Monday was Shannon's monthly appointment. By then the *Daily Democrat* had reported it was estimated that at the time of death Rick had the equivalent of three tranquilizers in his system, plus an assumed two bottles of beer and cannabis. There was no suggestion of foul play, but I figured the police were holding back information. During Shannon's monthly exam, I asked if he was expected at Moran's compound any time soon.

"Not for inside. But I got a standing gig painting exteriors. House is big. And lots of outbuildings. When I have a free day between jobs, I go up there and work. Write down my hours and leave it on the front porch under this weird wood sculpture he's got. Why you askin'?"

"I want you to do me a favor. Something we keep to ourselves."

"I *knew* you were hiding something about you and Moran. Remember I said so?"

"How about a hundred dollars for a few clicks of your phone?"
Shannon's blue eyes seemed to pop around in the sockets of his blotchy, heavy face. He gave his short brown ponytail a tug. "Like I said, why you askin'?"

"Are there times Bam and Sam aren't in a position to see if you're around the cars?"

"If I say yes, will you tell me what the hell's going on?"

A stale smell of cigarettes oozed from Shannon's pores. His eyes were glossy, like someone who'd had too much to drink the night before. Maybe every night before.

"Did you know Rick Fulton?"

"He did odd jobs at Moran's. You see them scars?"

I nodded.

"Woodrow," Shannon said. "A lot of vets got ripped off volunteering for screwy wars."

"I don't have evidence of anything. Just beginning an inquiry. One known only to you and me."

"If you think one of those gorillas trashed a vet, I'm in."

"Only if you're sure no one will see, it would help if you took pictures of the front grills of the Expedition and the Escalade. Does he have any other vehicles?"

Shannon's body moved with expectation. "There's a beige Honda SUV out there."

"Beige?"

"Yeah."

"Skip the Honda."

I told Shannon that once he took photos, he should create a disposable email address, and email the pictures to me. Immediately after I confirmed receiving them, Shannon should delete them from his phone and delete the disposable email account.

"You never know what someone might find. And don't think up reasons to go check out the cars. If I need anything more, I'll let you know."

Shannon twisted his inflated neck, trying to loosen it. "Those twins, his gofers? They call him Snake Face behind his back. It's chicken shit shameful." His face even redder than usual, Shannon hopped down from the examining table. "I'll go up there right now."

Normally a chatterbox, when Shannon left the clinic I didn't hear a word from him as he passed the front counter.

That afternoon I received a dozen photographs online showing vehicles and license plates. The Escalade showed nothing of note. The Ford Expedition had spots on the front fender. I couldn't make a guess as to what they were. No discernible dents. I downloaded the photos onto a USB stick; I didn't want to shoot them into the cloud. Soon as I got off work, I put the photos in email trash, and deleted all trash. I researched places to have them blown up, looking for somewhere outside of Sonoma County. No use taking a chance, no matter how slim, of my doings getting back to Moran. I found a place called The Lab, in Napa, called and played the doctor card.

"I'm Dr. Taylor. I could use your help. I hear you're the best at what you do." I'd never heard of the place. Even though it would be after regular business hours, I cajoled the fellow on the other end into meeting at The Lab, located in an industrial park away from Napa's swank side. It would take an hour and a half to get there.

Joel Holene, sole proprietor of The Lab, answered my door knocks. Soft spoken, his brown hair was long, thin. He radiated an aura of easy-going independence. Holene suppressed a laugh when I passed him the USB stick. I was led into a room with enough equipment to fly a Boeing 747.

Holene brought Shannon's pictures onto a screen that didn't seem connected to anything. He gave them a cursory run through. "Usually it's things like vineyards, drone shots of a winery, or customers want an image blown up to fit a particular wall. Some want old family pictures cleaned up. This is… let's call it exotic."

"If I assure you it's for a good cause, would that help?"

"Since you want the bumpers blown up, you're trying to see if these cars hit something. For a lawsuit? I probably shouldn't get involved."

"No. It's personal. You wouldn't be identified as printing the photographs."

It seemed curiosity got the better of him. "Let's see what I can find."

Holene asked me to give him in an hour. I drove to downtown Napa, had a burger topped with goat cheese, and walked a short while on a cement path along the river. A warm wind blew upstream. In early March, spring had come early. Summer was doing the same. Back at The Lab, I said no paperwork was needed and that I'd brought cash. I inquired about the bill and set money on the front counter. When I took the paper sack with the refined photographs and my USB stick, the bag had nothing on it to identify as coming from The Lab.

"I looked you up," Holene said. "Whatever you're getting yourself into, I'd appreciate anonymity. I'll lock the door behind you.'"

"Staying longer?"

"I have a little apartment in back. It's quite sufficient."

Holene walked me to the door and said goodbye.

I taped the photographs between small pieces of cardboard, wrote *Do Not Bend* in the lower left corner of a large envelope that had no return address. I did everything wearing blue surgical gloves so no fingerprints could be found, and pasted more stamps on the envelope than I estimated were needed. I dropped the package in a downtown Appleton mailbox at a little past one a.m.

After lunch, awaiting the next patient, my phone rang. Its face read Kendra. I stepped to the door, shut it gently, and answered.

"That couple's here. Thought you'd want to know."

"Do you think they finished shopping?"

In the background were clanging noises. "Probably not. They wouldn't leave a car full of food in the sun before they head out."

"Did you see what they're driving?"

"They parked in front. In a van with Something Furniture Moving on the side. They'll probably be here for like almost an hour. They tend to linger, like being in Appleton is like going to the big city." Kendra sighed. Her voice grew plaintive. "If you come in, can you pretend we don't know each other?"

"I won't be coming in. You've been very helpful."

I told Storm and Sandy I had to leave for the afternoon. At times we all covered for each other. In this instance, Storm snapped at me.

"I guess it doesn't hurt to be the boss's boyfriend."

That answered the question regarding if our colleagues had surmised the relationship.

"I'll make it up to you."

"You're right about that," Storm said.

Sandy shook her head. "You two," she said, and headed for her next appointment.

I went into Inez's office, said something came up and I was leaving for the afternoon. "Storm and Sandy will cover for me."

"What is it?"

"Remember the couple I talked about who came to the hospital when Kim Johnson was being operated on?"

"Their best buds. Live in the same area. I can't remember their names."

"Joan and Jim Finnegan. I've just been informed they're in Appleton, and will be for a couple of hours at a minimum. I'm going to go check their place out. Yeah, it's kind of a fishing expedition. But you never know what you might scare up."

Inez slipped off her glasses. She scratched an eyebrow. Then tore at it. "I'm not going to demand you don't go. We're not like that with each other. But if you can't reign yourself in soon, we got a big problem. Do you know how much that would hurt? And how it would look, right now, while we're trying to get people to donate?"

"I'll put in extra time, at night. Like I've been doing."

Inez flipped a hand toward her office door. "Just get out of here before I start screaming."

Mind sizzling, I headed north.

The delivery van belonged to the Finnegans?

I passed the address for the Finnegans I'd found in county

records, located a place to ditch my car. The gate to their place, comprised of redwood boards, was topped with barbed wire. To both sides ran barbed wire fences that looked identical to those at Kim and Rick's. I grabbed the top of a fence board, leaped and pulled myself up and swung my legs over the barbed wire like a pole vaulter. I fell sideways onto the ground.

After walking a couple of hundred yards down a dirt road, a dog barked. The barking grew louder. A Douglas fir forest thickened. There was more shadow than sunlight. Ahead were wood buildings, and the shrieking dog. It looked like an adult malamute. It charged. Its neck snapped and it flipped over as the chain collared to its neck reached its end. The dog squealed, regained its footing and barked nonstop, yanking on the chain.

A sack of dog food was near two steel buckets. I swept it up, jammed a hand inside, pulled out chunks of dog food and flung them past the malamute. Repeated this several times and set down the sack.

Moving fast, I looked under a tarp strewn far from what I assumed was the Finnegans' living quarters. Under it were nine sets of deer antlers, quite small to a couple of striking racks. To get to the cabin I'd need to pass the malamute, which munched away. That wasn't going to happen. In a large shed were an outboard engine, ropes, buoys and the like that I photographed. In a wood bin, under another tarp, pelts were stacked to above my knees, of deer and animals I didn't recognize.

The dog started up again. I raced to the food sack, hurled a handful of food past the snarling animal and got out of there, jogging the whole way. Going over the fence my half hand caught the barbed wire. After I picked myself off the ground I had to unhook a chunk of flesh from the underside of the wire strand. Holding the bleeding hand against the front of my shirt, I limped to my car and forced myself to not drive down Wathor Mountain like I was running away from something.

This second set of pictures came out clear enough, and damning.

Twenty-five

At work the next day, Inez asked about the bandage on my hand. I said I'd cut it on barbed wire at the Finnegans. Inez flashed a palm and looked away, telling me she didn't want to hear anymore.

Dale Hayes called from Los Angeles. She said they were looking to film *Love Speed* beginning on July nineteenth. That way actors under eighteen years old could finish before the school year began. Permits were in the pipeline. Would I be available?

"Anything I can do to help."

Thursday's dinner was the usual, me, my laptop and eating microwaved food at the coffee table that was in front of my one couch. It being June, the evening lingered. The phone rang. Carbone.

"Some interesting photographs arrived in the mail today. No return address, no note," he said. "They came to my house, not the substation."

"What are they of?"

"Cut the crap. Who else would anonymously send pictures of Moran's vehicles? Be straight with me. I'm straight with you."

"Are you? You've told me all you know about Moran's involvement in under-the-table commerce?"

Carbone's voice grew boomed in that popping gravel manner of his. "That tells me *you* know more than you're letting on."

I let those words float for a while, thinking about how I might reply.

Carbone shouted, "I watch over my territory in whatever ways are best for keeping the peace, and allowing citizens to live how they want. Some people aren't suited for regular life. That doesn't mean they're bad. They just can't play the games. You, on the other hand, are a meddlesome son of a bitch. Now I can't deal with things my way, not after you've sent me these pictures. You've got leverage on me. You can go talk to Wills again, tell him what you found. Wills, by the way, doesn't give a rat's ass about the people who live out in West County. He's a city kid."

I walked to the window that gave view of the apple orchard. It looked somewhat haunted in the fading light. "Don't you want to know if somebody helped Rick Fulton into that ravine?"

"On my terms, at my pace."

Looking at untrained apple trees, their branches merging with gossamer air, I added to the leverage Carbone had cited. "I'll tell you more of what you already know. And since I know, you'll have to deal with it. Jim and Joan Finnegan are running a poached animals operation on Wathor Mountain. Want to see some pictures."

I didn't mention driving their delivery van, transporting booty.

Carbone said, "I've given them till August first to phase things out. If you can manage to keep your mouth shut, I should be able to close down a few more things without people having to go to jail for making non-conventional choices. Choices driven by economic necessity."

"So you decide what's the law, and where it can be bent?"

"I thought I told you to cut the crap. Now, instead of letting Moran slowly hang himself, I got to go over there and have— what's he call it? I got to go have *social discourse* with the odd duck. An odd duck who's helped keep West County's economy operating for twenty years."

"Will you be bringing handcuffs?"

"I'll manage Moran. I'm asking you to give me two, three weeks to sort out things with people before you go to the department. And to be clear, I never received a nickel of Moran's money. Or anybody else's."

Carbone hung up.

That was the last time we talked. Early the next morning Carbone was found dead on Sunset Beach, in Sunset County, the next county north. He was in uniform. An eighteen-foot motorboat, stolen from a weekender's place near Timber Cove, smashed into rocks a few miles south of where the body was found. Unnamed sources told the *Daily Democrat* Carbone was rumored to have at times looked the other way if West County residents modestly grew pot for sale, poached game or otherwise made money outside the strictures of the law. An online article in the *Daily Democrat* described Carbone's thirty-eight years of public service. The sources further speculated Carbone, whose reputation as West County's moral and policing authority was at the core of his self-image, probably couldn't face a public reckoning. It would have destroyed him emotionally. An investigation, and autopsy, were forthcoming. The clinic was abuzz with chatter about Mayor Carbone.

I sat across from Inez, in her office with the door closed. "I don't buy a Carbone suicide any more than Rick Fulton drove himself off a cliff."

Inez shook her head. "Don't bring it to work. Go see your next patient." Inez blew strands of hair from her glasses in a way that was also a sigh. "No time to argue. I've got to prep for two Zooms with foundations."

"I hope they go great." I gulped, swallowed and said, "You're not going to like why I came in. I need to skip taking Bianca tomorrow. I'm sorry, I—"

Inez spoke over me. "You're going to stick your nose into Frank's passing, aren't you?"

I nodded.

Inez rose her shoulders, in a kind of stretch, then let them fall. "Frank did a lot of good. Of course I'm sorry he's gone. It's horrible. But it's police business, not health care." Not looking up, she said, "Do whatever you think you need to. You're going to do it no matter what I say, anyway."

Early the next morning I set out for Sunset County. A few miles past Jenner, the coastal highway commanded attention with hairpin turns.

Edwina, Rick, and now Carbone. I felt attached to all three. Their deaths needed to be run down. The county's investigations seemed to be crawling. And I needed to talk with Kim Johnson and Cliff Niles, who was the longtime sheriff of Sunset County.

Fourteen years before, Niles and I had tangled during my

last assignment as a private investigator. It involved a state senator, a local bad boy, the bad boy's sister and a few more locals, one of whom almost succeeded in choking me to death. I was remembering all that as I reached the redwood-sided Sunset County government complex on the inland side of Highway One. If things hadn't changed over the years, Niles would be in for a half day on Saturdays. If not I'd still poke around, see if I could find out anything about Carbone's demise.

I didn't call ahead because it would have given Niles an easy chance to avoid talking with me.

The parking lot was mostly empty. I rubbed my hands together against cold damp ocean air and walked to glass doors. They opened automatically. At a desk behind the front counter was a man, twenties, with longish brown hair that leaked from under a dark patrolman's cap, and vivid brown eyes. A name plate identified him as *Brian Benitez, Clerk*. He stood and nodded amiably.

"Can I help you?"

I extracted a Yates Health business card from my wallet. "I'm hoping to speak with Sheriff Niles. Does he happen to be in?"

Benitez stepped to the counter. I slid the little card under a low half circle opening in a Plexiglass barrier that wasn't there before Covid. He looked at the card, then at me. "Is he expecting you?"

"The opposite. Could you let him know I'm here?"

Benitez returned to his desk, lifted a black telephone receiver and looked at my business card as he pressed a button. Seconds later, the phone receiver was returned to its slot, and the Yates

Health business card was returned to me. I heard the sheriff's voice, still recognizable after those many years.

"Jeff Taylor, as I live and breathe."

Niles came down the hallway, right hand outstretched. He had the same greyhound rug hair, soft blue eyes that blinked a lot, and a round face the color of uncooked oatmeal. Yet he was remarkably different.

We shook hands. Niles looked me over. "You lost half your hair. Yes?"

"You lost half your stomach. More than half."

My guess was sixty pounds. On a five-nine frame, that much lost weight made Niles appear to have shrunk in the years between seeing him.

"A few trips to the ER with Afib can bring on a change in diet."

We walked on fawn-colored tiles. Niles looked over and up. "You passing through?"

"I wish. I'm here regarding an acquaintance of mine. Frank Carbone."

Niles stopped. "A genuine tragedy." Niles resumed walking. Our footsteps sounded in the empty hall, with Niles advancing in a kind of shuffle. It occurred to me that Niles was closer to seventy years old than sixty. "How did you come to know Sergeant Carbone? Last time I seen your name was when you stopped that mass shooting at Tahoe. The papers said you were a doctor."

I explained about working at Yates Health, bumping into Carbone at an accident site, said we'd become friendly, and left it at that.

"Small world," Niles said, "you landing next door in Sonoma County."

We reached a wood door with SHERIFF stenciled in white on it. Below that was taped a piece of paper with *Don't Knock* written on it. Niles opened the door inward. He gestured for me to enter, and pointed to a new-looking olive-green cloth swivel chair with adjustable armrests. He sat behind his desk. It was a mess.

Niles had a large square nose. He lifted it as though sniffing. "Tell me, what brings a former P.I., now a doctor, and me together on this fine morning?"

Niles bounced a little in his chair, and smiled. One aspect of Niles hadn't changed. He was a happy camper.

"No way Frank committed suicide," I said. "I talked to him Thursday night. A few times in the last two weeks, in person and on the phone. He sounded more like somebody interested in the future than in ending things."

"Does Sonoma County law know about these conversations?"

"I haven't quite gotten that far."

Niles' eyes twinkled. He rolled his chair backwards a couple of feet and slapped his right knee. "You're still a secretive one. No?"

I grinned to appease the man, and to maybe get more out of him that way. "You got me there."

Niles said, "What are you here for?"

I squeezed the fancy chair's armrests. "I'm thinking if Frank was going to drown himself, why steal a boat and motor twenty-four miles up to Sunset? The Sonoma coast has plenty of ocean to drown yourself in."

"Maybe he was thinking it over, cruising and thinking it over. Suicide is rarely an easy decision."

"You ever think about killing yourself?"

"Heck no," Niles said. "I'm happy with my career. Happy with the people I've known all these years."

I jumped in quick. "I remember you spoke of your wife with deep affection."

"As I ought to. She puts up with me."

"You know, you remind me of someone. Someone in terms of having a good marriage, a fulfilling life in a place he loved. He had a long career in law enforcement."

Niles rolled forward, grasped a corner of his desk. That was the only part of it not cluttered. He blinked half a dozen times. The lighthearted cheerfulness vanished. "Point taken. Now what do you think you can get from *moi*? You know I won't break the rules."

"Can you take me to where he was found? Then where the boat crashed?"

Niles lifted his police cap from the cluttered desk. We walked to the front counter without speaking. Niles spoke through the Plexiglass barrier. "Don't contact me unless it's an emergency. No dog bites. You got that?"

Clerk Benitez's voice dropped a couple of octaves from when I'd entered the building. "Yes, sir."

On the way to where Carbone's body was found, Niles stopped and bought two cups of hot coffee. At Sunset Beach, he introduced me to Deputy Seth Jacobs, who had spent the night in a Sunset County Range Rover watching an area of roped-off sand. Yellow police tape was draped around the ropes, which bobbed in the wind. Niles handed Jacobs a cup of steaming coffee.

To me, he said, "We're keeping this buttoned up on the off-chance a surprise comes along. Something that warrants further looking into. Dead center in the area is where he was found. Tide was high. Right now it's middling."

"Any indications of a struggle? Any marks on him? Even a bruise he could've picked up at home?"

"Clean as a whistle. The only mark on his whole body was where his right cheek was planted in sand until he was discovered. Otherwise, no chafe marks, no nothing."

"Who found him?"

"An older couple who takes pride in being first walkers of the day. Doris and Charlie Schmidt. Known them most of their lives."

Niles was patient. He let me wander around, look around. I really didn't have much to ask about. Next Niles took me to see an aluminum boat in the rocks at Oberti Point. Another Range Rover, and another deputy, this time a woman, fortyish, who sat on the front bumper.

"I feel bad for them," I said, "out in the cold all night."

"Bad?" Niles chuckled. "They're raking in time and a half, twelve hours a pop for sitting on their behinds." We reached the woman officer. She was introduced as Deputy Sharon Vallent. The coffee Niles handed her no longer emitted steam. He said, "You like these shifts, right? You like the solitude."

The deputy had jet black hair that blew in wisps from under her cap. "I like the extra income," she said.

Niles winked at me.

The roped off aluminum boat had dents in it. Its outboard motor had taken hits and was cockeyed.

Niles said, "We left it here, in case Sonoma County police want to do their own look-see. This morning comes a message asking to send pictures and a full report. I guess that means they think I know what I'm doing." To Vallent, Niles said, "Perry's Towing should be here by ten. Follow them till it's locked up, then bring me the key."

"Affirmative," said Vallent.

Niles said, "Perry's has a covered, lockable metal space. No one will touch that boat unless they're with me."

We headed back toward Sunset. The fog had retreated. Hints of blue sky pushed through here and there, creating bright spots on the heaving sea.

"How well did you know Carbone?" I asked.

"I'm embarrassed to say hardly at all. Our jurisdictions touched, yet we rarely made the effort to communicate with each other."

"Was that because he was a sergeant, and you're a county sheriff?"

Niles pulled into a wide spot on the side of the highway. At halting, the car bucked. Niles turned off the engine. He looked at me in a way that admonished. "You listen up, Mr. Jeff Taylor. I've been indulging your civilian poking around. I respect that you care, but you're too old to be the same cocky turkey you were fifteen years ago."

I looked out the window, to a hillside. Fog kept the grass there green. "I'm pissed off about Carbone. I'm pissed off about a lot of things."

I proceeded to tell Niles about Edwina, referring to her as Mystery Woman, the time we spent together and how it affected me. I skipped the returning spirit aspect.

"I read about it," Niles said. "That another secret? You and her?"

"I went to Santa Rosa the day after she got killed. Told the police what I just told you, with a few more details. I'm going to find who hit her, because the police seem to have forgotten it even happened."

Next I recounted Rick blasting into the clinic with Kim in his arms, the two half fingers in a bucket of ice, and racing to Memorial Hospital. Also the time spent with them on Wathor Mountain. I described his grotesque scars, his anger—two decades worth—and why I'd become hopeful Rick might turn his life around.

"He was supposed to meet with the police and a lawyer at department headquarters," I said, "to reveal a ring of poaching and other illegal activities. He never made it. I'm going to find who's responsible for Rick going over a cliff, and bring him in. I'm pissed off about all of it. When I'm pissed off like this, I act like an idiot."

During my recounting of events, Niles asked questions, nodded during my answers but did not offer opinions.

Telling Niles all that took almost half an hour. His seatbelt was long released, his chair tilted back like a chaise lounge.

Niles pressed a button and let down the driver's window. Fresh air and the scent of the Pacific Ocean joined us. "I can't help you, son."

Driving to Wathor Mountain I realized there was another reason, besides Carbone's death, that had compelled me to go to

Sunset County. With all that was going on inside me, I'd needed the presence of a steady hand. Someone to talk things through with. Sheriff Niles provided that. Inez was the only steady hand in my life, and she wasn't available for this.

I didn't blame her at all.

Twenty-six

Two cement barriers, the kind you see at highway construction sites, were placed at an edge of the road in the shape of a V. I parked, got out and peered over the cement blocks. Deep ruts scarred the cliff. Large boulders at the bottom had been smashed into pieces. That a crew had extracted a school bus from down there struck me as remarkable.

Oddly, there were no skid marks on the road, no ruts. Nothing to indicate Rick had attempted to avoid going over the side.

Was it possible somebody had taken a shot at him? Anything was possible, though nothing like that had been suggested in the newspapers or online.

The sagging gate of plastic pipes at Kim and Rick's homestead was, as expected, locked. I stood beside the Subaru, reached in and gave the horn three long honks. The temperature, inland and near the top of Wathor Mountain—more an extended hill than a true mountain—was twenty degrees warmer than along the coast. I peeled off my sweatshirt and tossed it onto the passenger seat.

This time it was a dusty purple Volkswagen Rabbit that topped the grade. It came to rest shortly before the gate. I grabbed my doctor's bag from the backseat. A woman, blonde with threads of gray, wearing a long-sleeved black top with fishnet sleeves and a long multicolored skirt, stepped out of the Volkswagen. Her vibe was neutral.

"Who are you?"

I held up the black bag. "Dr. Taylor. I'm here to check on Kim's fingers."

The woman's face relaxed. "I'm Nina. Kim says you saved her hand."

"Not me. The surgeon did."

"I assume you want in."

"If it's okay with Kim."

Nina reached into a sewed-on green corduroy pocket of her long skirt, found the large key and went to the gate. She slapped open the lock. We worked the gate open together.

Nina said, "We can leave it. I'm not paranoid like they are."

We got into the VW Rabbit. Nina reversed around on grass. We started down. The road was smoother than I'd have thought.

"How's she holding up?"

"One minute Kim's philosophical. She'll say it's god's plan. Later she'll say she and Rick are being punished for..." Nina's voice trailed off. "For stuff she won't talk about."

"I know about the poaching. No worries. That's not of concern to me."

Nina looked ahead with that neutral gaze. "She'll be glad you came. Other than the Finnegans, it's been just us living with Rick's ghost, so to speak."

"Is there anything you want to tell me privately, before I see her?"

"I already said about all there is to tell. I'm going stir crazy up here with a grieving widow. What the hell, they lasted almost twenty years. Given their life circumstances, they had a good run."

We didn't talk the rest of the way down a dirt road of a few hundred yards. Shale was packed where trees were thick, and the road would stay muddy during winter. At its end was a cleared area. An abandoned cabin, its roof covered with dark-green moss, was tucked under trees where the forest had not been logged. Where Nina stopped the land had been cleared. Nearby were a dirt-floored workshop, a firewood bin and a hand pump for well water. What stood out, though, were two smallish cabins. Each sported a porch with polished hand-hewn railings. Remembering the disorder inside the school bus, which I had at the time assumed Rick and Kim lived in, the tidy craftsmanship of the buildings stunned me. They also lent credence to Carbone's saying Rick was a good carpenter.

Nina cut the engine. Silence reigned over the landscape for untold miles. Smiling, Kim emerged from one of the cabins. She wore a white tank top and jeans. The homestead was profoundly serene and exhibited a pride in ownership. It was also where Kim had chopped off half of two fingers. A quarter mile down Wathor Mountain Road from the gate, Rick had crashed into oblivion. The contrast was gut wrenching, but I had duties to attend to and walked with Nina to where Kim stood on a covered porch.

Using the hand without a fingers cast, Kim gave one of her shy waves. "Thanks for coming." She giggled, put out her left hand to shake. Her pupils were dilated as wide as nickels. The musky scent of pot was unmistakable.

"I thought you went straight."

Kim played with a blonde ponytail. She giggled again, sounding loopy. "This is just till I accept it. To get through the rough patches."

Nina threw me a look that correlated with her annoyance.

On the covered porch were two wood chairs of a homemade variety.

"I'll get the cleaning things," Nina said.

"I have what we need."

Without a word, Nina went inside the cabin Kim hadn't emerged from.

I pulled one of the chairs close to the other, sat and set the black bag on the plank decking. Kim sat. She seemed embarrassed at being caught high on pot.

"How are you holding up?"

"Rick was my whole world."

"And you were his."

"Don't make me cry. I don't want to cry anymore."

"Let's have a look at those fingers."

I motioned for Kim to offer her hand, then removed the cast. The stitches were beginning to dissolve. They needed tending to. The fingers and inside of the cast were less than sanitary. I asked Kim to raise the two fingers. They were not as swollen as before. It looked like she got an eighth of an inch in upward movement, about the same as at the earlier visit. Pulling them downward Kim made what looked like maybe a quarter of an inch. It required effort.

I instructed Kim to take the cast off once in the morning and once in the afternoon, an hour each time, and to be sure to keep it on whenever sleeping.

"Besides you, who did Rick see during his last days?"

"Joan and Jim. We see them all the time." Kim shivered. "He went down to Mr. Moran's the night before. Said he had to warn him about something."

"Warn him?"

"Rick said the roof on his garage was about to collapse."

"You can't show Moran a roof in the dark."

"I knew it wasn't true. Rick was always trying to protect me."

I attended to Kim's hand. It caused her discomfort. I used Q-tips dipped in disinfectant on the inside of the small cast, stroking every centimeter. Once finished I returned the cleaning items to the doctor's bag.

"What kind of shape was Rick in when he left? The last time. Was he okay to drive?"

Kim closed her eyes, shook her head. "I… Uh… He drove bombed a hundred times."

I kept my gaze away from Kim, thinking it might make it easier for her to talk. "Do you think anyone could have caused the wreck?"

There was silence in Kim's paradise that had turned, perhaps, into a prison. "I don't know. I don't want to know."

"Okay." I slowly ventured into what I planned to say. "By now you know I know about the salmon, the abalone. The venison, everything. It adds up to serious trouble with the police."

I looked over. Kim's voice quaked. "It doesn't matter anymore."

"Maybe not for Rick, but for others it could matter a great deal. Like for Alex Moran. Like for the Finnegans. Like for you."

"Please don't." Tears rolled downward.

"You have to get rid of everything. As in right after I leave. The diving equipment. Whatever storage stuff you used. Anything written. Anything remotely related. It won't be long, and the police are going to show up here."

Kim nodded. The tip of her nose now red, her cheeks wet, she spoke to feet. "Am I in trouble?"

"Not yet. Your only chance is to get rid of any possible evidence as fast as you can. Don't stash it anywhere on your land. It'll be found."

More nodding. "Where?"

"The best thing would be to tie rocks around everything, have someone go as far out in the ocean as possible, and dump it." I slowed, giving Kim time for her thoughts to keep up. "I don't think you'll be thrown in jail, but the fines will be huge if you're caught. I figure they'd put you on probation, you know, for a few years. But that's just my guess. The only thing I'm sure of is the police will come calling."

"Finnegans have a boat," Kim whispered. "That's what Rick used."

"Call them. Save yourself. You have access to a cell phone?"

"Dr. Taylor," Kim said, sniffing, wiping her face. With ponytails in rubber bands dangling to both sides, she appeared extremely young. Extremely young and extremely stoned. "Please go. I'll make the calls, get rid of everything. Then I'm leaving. I'm moving in with friends in San Jose. They'll make sure I see a good doctor."

We said goodbyes. I walked up the road to my car. Something not noted on the drive down were small red reflectors embedded into edges of the road on turns. They'd show when driving the road at night. Based on the mess inside the school bus, I'd completely underestimated decorated army veteran Rick Fulton.

Driving down Wathor Mountain, I changed my plans and decided not to stop and confront the Finnegans. Bianca and Inez were leaving for Inez's parents' house in Salinas the next morning. I wanted to have some time with Bianca before they left. Maybe we'd shoot some hoops at the nearby elementary school before our last shared dinner for a month.

Sunday afternoon, naked, in bed at my place. Inez had returned from dropping off Bianca in Salinas. We seemed to fill every square foot of that tiny room. We did not make love. I talked about going to Sunset County and seeing where Carbone had washed ashore. That he had no marks on him indicating a struggle. That it didn't make sense for Carbone to steal a boat and travel north to jump in the ocean. I described the spot where the school bus crashed. Then the visit with Kim, and her telling me Rick drove down the mountain to Moran's the night before the crash, claiming he needed to warn him about a garage roof that was about to collapse.

"Rick and Carbone's deaths are both fishy. Why are the police acting so blasé about them?"

Inez grabbed the brown top she'd worn on the drive from Salinas. She pulled it overhead, tugged her tresses through its neck opening. "I did some thinking on the way home. Our conversation confirms my thoughts."

"Meaning?"

"I get four weeks a year to slow down. Four weeks a year to not have to single parent Bianca."

Reaching under the blanket, I squeezed Inez's hand. Squeezed it again.

She said, "You're obsessed with these tragedies. They don't have anything to do with you."

"I disagree with the second part."

She let go of my hand. "I have to think through if it's in my best interest, and Bianca's, to be with you."

"I don't like where this is going."

"Me, either." Inez took my hand again. "I need a break from us. I've been going ninety miles an hour all year. I have to slow down, or I'll crash. The way you are with these deaths, it's not healthy for us."

I turned onto my side; Inez did the same. My arm wrapped around her waist. Inez clutched my hand.

My words came in an uncomfortable whisper. "Did you just break up with me?"

"I need to put things on pause."

"A pause sounds a lot like breaking up."

"All I know for sure," Inez said, "is if I don't slow down, and you don't slow down, we're going to be a train wreck."

PART THREE

Twenty-seven

The converted garage seemed even smaller than before. My footsteps were heard individually. The sparse furnishings confirmed my isolation from others once I left work. Cheerful sounds of a summer gathering on the other side of the apple orchard were not bearable. I went to Edwina's tree abode but didn't experience its usual comforts.

Days at the clinic were less awkward than expected. With staff and patients hurrying about, Inez and I didn't cross paths much. Suzanne was the only person who sensed something afoul. Between patients she came into my examining room and shut the door. Her tall Afro shined under banks of old fluorescent lights.

"If you need to talk, it'll be private. Any time after hours."

I assured Suzanne I was fine.

The week passed slowly. Friday's dinner was takeout chicken burritos from Ochoa's, eaten without bothering to use a plate. On my laptop the Giants played the Dodgers in Los Angeles. Ohtani slapped a double down the right field line, driving in two runs and giving the Dodgers the lead. Knuckles rapped the only door. I hoped it was Inez, knew it wouldn't be, and worried it might be Moran's twin tough guys. Standing behind the locked door, no nearby windows to see outside through, I asked who was there.

"Don Wills, Sonoma County Sheriff's."

No one would make that up. I unlocked the door, swung it open. In uniform, Lieutenant Wills stepped into the living room looking around as if searching for something in particular. Seeing the laptop and wadded paper napkins in front of the couch, he sat without invitation in the chair facing it. He watched me sit across from him.

"I believe you have access to photographs of interest to the department. We'd like to take a look."

I turned the sound down and took a leisurely look at the baseball game, slowing things on purpose, to show Wills he wasn't going to run the show. "What photographs are you referring to?"

"Ones of Moran's cars that showed up in Sergeant Carbone's mailbox. The day before he disappeared, he told me you two talked about them."

"I parked way up the road, hiked down through the woods and took some pictures," I said, keeping Shannon out of it. "Moran's car's bumpers. I thought Mayor Carbone might find them intriguing. They're not among his effects?"

Wills had made a face at hearing the nickname *Mayor Carbone*. "They're missing. I'm asking you to give me what you have. Voluntarily."

"I don't like it that when Frank and I were in frequent communication, he turns up dead. You're going to have to tell me more about Frank's death, or get a search warrant."

Wills leaned forward. His brown eyes sparked. "Frank confessed to knowing about illegal goings on in West County he'd let pass. He handled things his own way. I'm not saying that was okay, or it was always bad. But we have two dead bodies out there. We—"

I interjected, "Three dead bodies. You neglected Mystery Woman."

"I'm focused on Carbone, Rick Fulton, and any illegal activities that may be related to their deaths."

"What if the three are related?"

"Then it'll turn up. Now let's have a look at the pictures."

Again, I slowed matters, gathering soiled napkins, going to the kitchen and dropping them in the plastic trash container under the sink. From there, I said, "After you tell me if you think Frank committed suicide."

"I investigate. I don't speculate."

"Respectfully, that's bull. Of course you have thoughts about what might have happened."

Wills smiled. The smile was as thin as his mustache.

Carbone had known about Edwina's tree abode. Did he tell Wills about it? Carbone knew about the illegal food and, logically speaking, knew about it being delivered. Did he know about me in that regard? How much more did Wills know than he was revealing? I was on guard to not talk myself into a corner.

"If we obtain a search warrant," Wills said, "it will be for your house, your car, and Yates Health. It would be a shame to have to make you look bad in front of your coworkers."

I returned to the couch. "It would be a shame for the police to look like they're harassing people at a public health clinic."

Loud knocking rattled the entry door. "Hey Doc, we got to talk."

I hollered, "It's unlocked. Come on in."

Shannon entered forcefully. He stopped dead in his tracks at seeing a policeman in uniform. "Woodrow." His red eyes seemed about to pop out of their sockets. "I mean…" Shannon said nothing more.

I hadn't gotten around to buying chairs for the teak dining table, so there was no place for Shannon to sit.

Wills stood. "Nice to meet you, Woodrow." He stepped to Shannon, whose feet seemed glued to the floor. "Don Wills, Sonoma County Sheriff's Department."

Wills offered his right hand. Shannon shook it. He looked a little drunk and utterly confused.

"My name's… Hey, I didn't see another car."

Wills took a visual inventory of the new arrival. "I left it in the lot at Forester Park. No use stirring up neighborhood gossip with a police car in front of someone's house."

Unsure of how to manage matters with Wills, I was glad for the interruption. I knew I'd eventually have to give up the photographs, at least those of Moran's cars because they were known to Wills, and possibly pictures of the Finnegans' operation—which I was glad to do but wanted to first find out if they were connected to the three deaths that were gnawing at me.

Wills turned from Shannon, nodded to me. "We'll continue this tomorrow. Ten a.m., my office?"

I remained on the couch. "Anything I can do to help."

Passing Shannon, Wills looked at him like he was trying to

remember something. The lieutenant closed the door on his way out.

Shannon let out a beery exhale. "What the hell was that about?"

"He wants me to give him the photos of Moran's cars."

Shannon paced with his mouth open. He worked his log-like neck around. "What've you got me into?"

"Nothing. I told him I took the pictures. Said I snuck into Moran's compound, took the pictures and mailed them to Carbone."

"I need a beer."

"Tell you what," I said. "Take a seat, calm down. We'll have a beer together. One beer."

Going to the refrigerator I heard another of Shannon's loud exhales. I opened two bottles, went to the living room and handed one to Shannon. He downed half of it before sitting on the chair.

"What's the occasion for your visit?"

"The occasion is some weird shit's been going down at Moran's."

"Like what?"

"More pictures. I created another fake email account. Before I send them, you should do the same. Now that I've seen a cop here, no way I'm sending anything to your regular email. They can force you to show 'em. They can even retrieve deleted ones."

"Good idea. What are we hiding?"

Shannon finished the beer in two gulps. He hesitated to set the bottle on the coffee table. I set my bottle on its badly scratched surface. Shannon eyed his bottle for any remaining beer, found none and set the bottle down.

"So, I'm up there painting. Weekends are good because you usually can't work weekends in people's houses. It's their down time. Moran's is a no-down-time kind of place."

"From what I can tell, he stirs a lot of different pots."

Shannon said, "I'm up on this ladder, painting the eaves. The Expedition rolls in. Sunlight bounces off the front bumper. It's obviously new. Sam climbs out, heads inside. Before he comes back, I click pictures, put away the phone. Both brothers come out. Sam backs up half a circle to outside the garage. Bam follows. He comes out of the garage with a bucket. Two sponges float in it. I don't know what's in the water, but they wear gloves to the elbows and scrub all the bumpers and door handles with it." Shannon couldn't stay still. He got up and paced the room. "I keep brushing the eaves, don't look over. I hear a hose turn on. Long and short, when they go back in the house all the bumpers and crap look the same. They scrubbed the newness off the new bumper. I zoomed and took what I could. Tell me what you think. Hey, can I have one more? Just one?"

"No."

Shannon stopped pacing. "I think maybe they did Fulton. He was a survivor. You saw them scars."

"What's your evidence? If the police find spent bullets in the vicinity, say, that's a possibility. Something must have scared him off the road. But what? The scene was without anything resembling a confrontation. The road has no skid marks."

"All I know is, that guy doesn't drive himself over a cliff. Something made him."

Shannon resumed pacing while I created a fake Yahoo account. I looked through the photos he emailed. They weren't great but they were good enough. The first two, angling down at the black Ford Expedition parked not far from the house, showed what was clearly a new front bumper. The others, with the car parked perpendicular to the garage, showed it had been washed. The pavement was wet. The visible portion of the front bumper no longer shined. It looked the same as the visible part of the back bumper and the door handles.

"Do you have any idea what they used?"

"Only that it was strong enough they wore gloves."

"Don't go up there for a while. We don't want them knowing they're under suspicion."

Shannon's nod seemed reluctant. I scooped his empty beer bottle from the coffee table. Shannon worked his thick neck side to side.

"Thanks for these," I said. "Next moves are up to me. Oh," I added, "if Lieutenant Wills somehow knows you spend time at Moran's, and brings you in for questioning, you're a house painter. You go there because Moran pays well. You never took any pictures."

Shannon walked to the door. "I'm just a barn owl with a paint brush."

Twenty-eight

Wills, in civilian clothes, was at the sheriff department's main entrance when I arrived at ten Saturday morning. I had the original USB stick in a front pocket. A copy was in Appleton, taped to the underside middle of the teak dining table. The sheriff department's hallways were even quieter than on my other visit. A custodian mopped the floor.

Wills had donuts waiting on paper plates, steaming coffee, cream and sugar packets. I declined the food and drink but gestured for Wills to enjoy them.

"You're missing the best in town," he said, and brought a maple donut to his mouth.

I had three sets of incriminating pictures: the first bumper ones on the USB stick; the poaching operation at the Finnegans; the before and after bumper pictures Shannon had taken the day before. I could relinquish the first set without incriminating myself in the illegal food business. Wills could work from there. A visit to Moran's, to check out his vehicles, would show the current front bumper was a different one than in the original photographs.

Wills took another bite of maple donut, swallowed. "Do you want me to say please?"

I handed over the USB stick. Wills set it away from the sweets and coffee. "I did a little digging," he said. "Your friend's name isn't Woodrow. It's Shannon Lunge. I got it from his license plate number."

"Woodrow's this odd thing he says sometimes. It's like he burps it out."

"When he's nervous?"

"I can't say."

"Why not?"

"Because I don't know what it means."

"Is he a friend of yours?"

"More of a patient. We're informal at Yates. It takes more time, but it's worth it in terms of long-haul results."

"And you've been at Yates for?"

"It's coming up on a year."

"I see. You've gotten long haul results in less than a year." Wills nodded, scoring his point.

"I'm following what I observe my colleagues do. Everyone goes the extra mile. Shannon is on the high maintenance end of patients."

I wouldn't mention Shannon helping me get the dining table at Odin's, and mentally checked boxes about what else not to say.

Wills put the food and drink atop a gray metal filing cabinet, wiped fingers on a white napkin he also set there. He slid open the filing cabinet's top drawer, removed a laptop; its cord was wrapped around it. Without saying anything, Wills plugged in the laptop, fired it up, inserted the USB stick into a side port. He clicked through the blown-up images.

"Why go to Moran's and take pictures of his cars?"

"As you know, I had a kind of doctor-patient friendship with Mystery Woman. I don't see the police making any progress on who hit her. It seems like the whole thing has been dropped."

"You're good at talking, Dr. Taylor. You're not as good at answering questions." Scents of coffee and sweets circulated in the compact office. "For what purpose did you take these photographs? Maybe I missed it."

I stood, reached my arms overhead. "This is a very uncomfortable chair."

"So I've been told."

I dropped to the wood seat. "I met Frank Carbone when Mystery Woman was killed. Met him at the scene. We hit it off. You know, I'm a doctor asking if anybody needs medical attention. He'd heard about me making house calls all over West County. Frank was upset. He said the victim appeared to be only in about her twenties. I asked if he had any idea of who in the area might have a big black car like the witness described. He mumbled a whispered, 'fucking Moran.' Caught himself, cleared his throat. I couldn't let it go."

Carbone wasn't around to refute my claim; I figured I was safe.

Wills, clicking through the pictures a second time, used his left hand to pluck at his mustache like he was plucking notes on a harp. He made a few more clicks, probably logging off, and looked up. "Frank wouldn't have said that to you. I still say you're hiding something. Thanks for coming in."

There were too many somethings I was hiding to count before Wills had me out of his office, including that Mystery

Woman, Edwina Seeba, was some kind of spirit. Walking down the hallway, alone, my armpits were damp, my cheeks hot.

The valley between Santa Rosa and Appleton was broad. Far ahead were green, tree-covered West County hills. I thought about how everyone involved in what Wills would become immersed in had hidden something incriminating and/or of significance. Odin hid from Moran that he couldn't drive the delivery route. Rick hid that he was poaching. The Finnegans hid their poaching. The Finnegans hid that they'd drugged me; there were no other candidates. With Moran it was the replaced bumper and orchestrating the deliveries of illegal foodstuffs. Common sense indicated that the well of his hidden acts was drilled deeper. Frank Carbone had hidden crimes from the crime stoppers themselves. As for myself, the most significant thing I was hiding was how frightened I was that I'd permanently lose Inez. Nothing had ever scared me more.

That afternoon I walked to Appleton High School, near downtown. I jogged eight laps on a red, rubbery track. Next I ran the length of the synthetic football field, stopped in the end zone and did thirty push-ups. Ran back and did thirty push-ups. Did this until I could only trot the hundred yards and eke out fifteen push-ups. This was the best way I knew to tamp down an overly stimulated mind.

Walking a cool-down lap, my phone sang. It was Odin. I crossed the track and sat in aluminum bleachers. Sunlight bounced off them, reminding me of Shannon's photos of the new front bumper on Moran's Ford Expedition.

"Your stitches must be rags by now," I said. "How bad do they smell?"

"No smell at all, because they're gone," Odin said. "For like awhile now."

"How'd it happen?"

"Mr. Moran. Said he felt bad about his guys going too far that time. Said he wanted to make up for it."

I didn't think Moran felt bad about that or anything else. "How much are you into him for now?"

"Nothing." Odin's voice was perky. "Mr. Moran made arrangements with a doctor in Ukiah. He did it as a gratuity."

"You mean he did it gratis."

"That's what I said."

"Whatever." I pictured Odin, the big head topped with a straw hat, the piano keys teeth, a kind of lumbering walk. Not the sharpest tool in the box. "Every time you call, you want something. What's on today's menu?"

"Info. Mayor Carbone called me the day before he was found on the beach. He talked in circles, saying I shouldn't be in contact with who he called 'certain individuals.' Said changes were coming soon. Said he wanted to give me a heads up."

"What does that have to do with me?"

"If the police come sniffing around, you and I should make sure our stories match."

"I've purchased a lamp, a side table and a dining room table from you. What does that have to do with the police?"

"You don't have to pretend with me," Odin said.

"By what you're saying, you must have me mixed up with someone else. Goodbye."

I disconnected. It seemed I'd become popular, receiving phone calls and even visitors. That did not strike me as a good omen.

The *Daily Democrat* reported Mrs. Sheila Carbone, and the Accomazzo Funeral Home and Mortuary, in Appleton, estimated attendance at Carbone's service would be anywhere from two to three hundred. Coupled with his growing up in the lower Russian River area, it was decided to hold an outdoor gathering at Wallen Meadow Park, which touched the river. Carbone's wife was quoted as telling the article's reporter, "We're planning a get together of Frank's people. To remember him. We're not calling it a celebration of life. His passing isn't something to celebrate." She added, "We ask everyone to carpool."

Arriving an hour early, I wasn't the first person there. Caterers were setting up tables, carrying buckets of ice and bottled water. Already in place were rows of wood chairs longer than rows of pews in most churches. White umbrellas sprouted above the tables, which were being loaded with food. A warm Sonoma County summer day was freshened by an upriver breeze.

I situated myself well behind the food tables and rows of seats, under a drooping willow tree. A woman and a man set up a microphone on a portable wood stage. People came in waves. First were West County folks, no suits, no ties. Knowing it would be a lengthy event, most wore hats to protect themselves from the sun. Many women were sheathed in colorful scarves. A love-fest, people greeted each other with kisses, calls of affection and lavish hugs. An older woman who I guessed was Mrs. Carbone, wearing a black hat, was surrounded by well-wishers.

Inez arrived with Suzanne, Storm and Sandy, who at work I called The S Squad. I'd never seen Inez in a skirt. She glowed in magenta, not her trademark brown. Soon as Inez entered the central lawn area, adjacent to the chair rows, people broke from conversations to hail her, and hug her. I ached to join them but was not part of their tribe. Observing the enormity of Inez's world compared to mine struck me like a whack on the head.

Kurt Sanderson was there, wearing a baseball cap. He talked quietly with people I didn't recognize. Joan and Jim Finnegan arrived. In Joan's hair were three bright peacock feathers. Jim wore vintage spectacles with clip-on sunglasses. They were relaxed, shaking hands and exchanging embraces with the younger West County folks in attendance, younger being anyone under forty.

The police arrived en masse. A final wave consisted of officialdom, mayors, members of the county Board of Supervisors led by West County's Nanette Hapkins, Congressman Tillman, and others I didn't recognize. It was an unusual blending of authority figures and those who rejected most systems of authority. It was West County.

Supervisor Hapkins took the stage. She thanked everyone for coming, then thanked half a dozen people by name. The tributes commenced. Overwhelmed by my separateness from the others I retreated down a path in riparian brush, to be alone by the river. Moran stood at water's edge in his habit of black turtleneck, black jeans, black running shoes. His dyed helmet hair didn't budge in wind that increased where funneled at a narrow spot in the river valley. Moran stared into the water like he was reading tea leaves. He and I were perhaps the only people taking respite from the love-fest. That we shared anything at all made me queasy.

Moran turned. He put his hands in front pockets. The river, slow in summer, made a gentle swishing sound. Its waters appeared somewhere between a cloudy gray and a muted green. Nearby brush smelled as fresh as the whispering river. Moran reverted to surveying its slow-moving surface.

"You interest me," he said.

"Why?"

"Because you are interested in me."

"You influence a lot of people. You have sway over them. That's interesting."

Moran produced a black wallet. From it he extracted a business card and passed it to me without making eye contact.

"A week from today," Moran said. "High noon. You are welcome to join a Session."

"How much?"

Moran's tongue made its snake-like appearance not once but twice.

"You ask how much?" The tone of Moran's clipped voice summarily dismissed the subject. "Zero. It would be my pleasure to welcome you aboard. Instructions are on the card."

I folded the business card in half. Walking away, I waved it overhead. "I'll think about it."

Rather than return to the gathering for Carbone, I drove to SunSpot and sneaked down to Edwina's tree-trunk house. Stretched out on the tan blankets, I wondered if I should tell Inez everything. Throw myself at the mercy of her court to justify my obsessions. I turned the subject over and over in thought, finally deciding it would be cowardly to angle for her love by admitting poor decisions and reviewing my excessive stubbornness.

That night, searching the Sessions website, I came upon: *Next Saturday, noon. 21 placements available.*

Twenty-nine

A fternoons and evenings passed slowly. Toast-colored summer grasses struck me as barren. On Friday I sent a message to the email account that posted the announcement regarding the upcoming Session. I asked for a brief private conversation afterward.

The reply: *I choose to grant your request.*

Saturday's gathering at Moran's was heralded by an elevated string of Tibetan prayer flags: blue, white, red, green and yellow. I followed half a dozen cars on an asphalt road, most accurately described as pristine, to a flat parking area with grass trimmed as short as a golf course fairway. Neither the black Expedition nor Escalade were in view. Rather than leave my phone in the car, as instructed, I'd turned off the sound and left it in an oversized pocket of hiking shorts. About twenty people carried a yoga mat and water bottle, as did I. Lines formed outside two outdoor concrete block bathrooms, like you'd see at a park. The online instructions were that once you stepped inside the meeting hall, there were no restroom breaks. People nodded, friendly like, yet subdued. No one spoke. Coming out of the bathroom I was face-to-face with Kurt Sanderson. He smiled approvingly.

Near the entrance to a large redwood building were more prayer flags. Inside, the only light came through four skylights worked into a wood ceiling. The walls Shannon had painted were a spooky marine blue. Sprinkled across the floor were white plates topped with black masks like those used to aid in sleeping. Everyone found a spot, took off shoes, unrolled yoga mats. Joan and Jim Finnegan settled in at both sides of an ornately carved baronial chair tucked against a wall. I saw the custom was to go flat on your back, arms to both sides, forming a cross.

Moran entered. The room grew utterly soundless. He wore black over black, and black socks. He lowered himself to the floor, turned onto a side, took hold of an ankle and slowly pulled his leg upward until it made a ninety-degree angle to his torso. Everyone followed suit as best as they and I could. Moran rolled over, lifted the other leg. This was followed by a fifteen-minute regimen that seemed a combination of yoga, Pilates and things I didn't recognize, but everyone else in the room seemed to know by heart. Moran was so limber as to seem boneless. Without prompting, attendees donned their masks and went flat, arms out. This was followed by about fifteen minutes of rhythmic breathing, verbally conducted by the host.

Notably different than the clipped, computer-sounding voice I was accustomed to, Moran's words were delivered honey-smooth. After the breathing, Moran's voice moved as he slowly walked about in the meeting hall.

"You are not yesterday. You are not tomorrow. You are not today. You are."

I thought: *Three hundred and fifty bucks for this?*

On the other hand, Moran's voice was genuinely comforting.

"Without the distraction of looking, now you can choose to see. Forget I, you, me, them. Those concepts occupy space in your mind. In return for letting them invade your thoughts, what do you receive? The concepts of me and you as separate, what do they offer? You already are what you are. Know it."

A low, congregation-like affirmation: "Know it."

It was easy to let words wash over me and not think about what Moran was saying. It was easy to let Moran's words make music and leave it at that. I caught myself falling into a light sleep, and came awake confident I hadn't snored.

As Moran's voice traveled about the room, I imagined a candle doing so. The candle in my mind spoke. "Attempting to separate yourself from others, trying to understand who you are not, is clutter. See? Pick up the litter in your head. Throw it away. Cleanse your interior streets."

I thought of Miley and her Hefty bag harvesting of litter on Ridge Road, which made me wonder where Moran got his material. I suppressed a laugh. And thought of how sincere the other attendees were.

"People talk about going to outer space as if that means something. It does not. We already are in outer space. There is nowhere to go. We are already there. Here. Know it."

"Know it," came the refrain.

And so it went. It felt good to be among people who shared something, though exactly what it was they shared I didn't understand. I did sense their kinship. A few times I heard the shuffling of feet; twice, near me, I thought I heard footsteps. Maybe I wasn't the only restless one in the group. At hearing car sounds I wondered if Bam and Sam had returned.

Matters took a strange turn when Moran began telling a story about who he termed, "a new friend." In his telling it sounded like a church homily.

"He was raised in a small village near the sea, by a single parent. He grew tall. He became a star basketball player."

I squirmed, barely able to keep myself on the yoga mat as Moran continued to reel off what anyone could find about me on the internet. Stifling a desire to leave, under the mask I sweated heavily. Would people understand Moran was talking about me? How could they not after he described the slicing of my hand in a workplace accident?

I tried to block out his words. And failed.

Moran said, "This man overcame all of that to become a doctor. He serves souls." The voice passed me. I heard a sound like from creaking wood. Again, I thought I heard car sounds.

"You may now unmask."

I tore off the mask, blinked against new light, found the white plate to my right and set down the mask. I looked around. The meeting hall was empty except for Moran and I, and the plates were covered with black masks. For some reason they reminded me of cemetery gravestones. Moran sat on the massive chair. Arrows were carved in the wood above his head. From the visit to Wathor Mountain I recognized the handiwork of Rick Fulton.

I sat up, reached for my running shoes, slipped them on. "That wasn't funny."

Moran smiled benignly. His posture was flawless.

"Where is everybody?" I asked.

"People are where they are. You indicated a desire for social discourse."

Anger brewed the familiar steam in my head that came with being pissed off. I suppressed that anger, ran a hand into a pocket of the oversized hiking shorts and clicked my phone so it recorded at its highest volume. I'd practiced all week.

I kept my eyes on Moran, trying to gauge his reactions. "I'm curious. You have a lot of people doing your bidding, in one way or another, and nothing touches you. Do you think you can break the law and stay untouchable?"

Moran sat comfortably in a full lotus on his polished wood throne. "Let me ask you something. Have you ever done things another person might consider wrong? Even break the law?"

"I don't make it a habit, but I've broken rules for a good cause. What would turn you into a law breaker?"

"Is there any more important a cause than personal choice?"

I rolled up the yoga mat and tied it off. The kettle in my head whistled with steam. "Your personal choice is just selfishness dressed up in a catchy phrase."

I stood.

Moran glided down, stood in front of the ornate wood chair. "There is no such thing as selfishness if you are following destiny."

I stepped around mask-covered plates, which suddenly seemed ridiculous, toward the door. Moran—quick as a cat—cut me off. I both wanted to bolt and wanted to pummel him. I both wanted to get him riled up, and talking, and get myself out of there before Bam and Sam showed up.

Yoga mat cradled against my side, I said, "What is it you believe in? Believe in enough it guides your life."

The snake tongue appeared and disappeared. "I believe in freedom."

"You believe in taking. I think you'd take a person's life and not feel a thing. You're that low."

Moran's expression did not change. "Who are you to be the judge of me?"

"I'm leaving now. Step aside."

"My choice is to not step aside. You are to tell me what you think you know."

"My choice is this."

I dropped the rolled tight yoga mat and slapped Moran's mouth so hard his knees crumpled like a folding chair. His butt smacked the wood floor. Moran looked up. His expression still did not change. It occurred to me that his green swami eyes were a kind of mask, that his words were another kind of mask, and that deep down inside Alex Moran was an empty vessel.

He put fingers to his mouth. He looked at them. They were bloody, with tiny speckles of face powder that reminded me of a child's glitter.

I wove my way past black masks, to the door.

Moran called across the airy meeting hall. "I choose to keep my freedom over losing it over someone who no longer exists."

"Did you just tell me you hit Mystery Woman? That you were the driver?"

"Know it. And no one will ever be able to prove it. Now get off my land."

Thirty

I drove the immaculate black asphalt to Ridge Road and turned right at the Tibetan prayer flags. Drove Ridge Road, and down Bishop's Grade almost to the coast highway, parked and listened to the recording. For the only time I could recall, anger had worked for me rather than against me.

I wanted to drive to Inez's house and tell her about the strange and exotic Session, including how for much of it I'd felt comforted. Of course this was not a good idea. Instead, when I got home I did at little prep work, then called Lieutenant Wills. We agreed to meet at the sheriff's department headquarters at six-thirty.

He didn't speak as we walked the hallway to his office, where Wills gestured for me to take the uncomfortable wood chair that poked its occupant in the back.

"Sorry to interrupt your family again on a weekend," I said.

No reply. Wills took out his phone, set it next to a closed notebook. Like before, Wills asked if he could record our conversation.

"Anything I can do to help."

Wills tapped his phone a few times. He identified himself by name and rank, gave the date, time and location of the interview.

I sensed Wills was tougher than he appeared, that he was one of those guys who can flip a switch and cause damage.

"Do you have any reason to believe you should have an attorney present?"

"As said before, I don't need one."

Wills opened the notebook. He flipped past a few pages with writing on them. "For your sake, I hope you are correct. Now, tell me about today. Then, if you volunteer to, play the conversation with Alex Moran you described during your phone call to me this afternoon."

Before going to Santa Rosa, my preparation had included sending the photos taken at the Finnegans to a fake email account; deleting them from my phone; deleting every message involving Carbone, received and sent; deleting notes concerning Edwina. I experienced the buzz I'd felt working for Sherman Investigations, in my twenties. I was on the hunt.

I finished my description of the Session. Wills stopped recording. When I played Moran's words about how no one could prove anything, Wills recorded them.

"You realize this doesn't necessarily mean much legally, right?"

"To me it sounds like enough to build a case on. By the way, did you get a search warrant for Moran's bumpers?"

"Since in this county search warrants are in the public domain, I'll save you time. I won't discuss how it went, but now his guard is up."

"Anything further on Mystery Woman, or Carbone? It seems like nothing's happening."

"These things take a lot more time than people realize. Considering your background, I'd think you'd be aware of that."

"How much can you tell me about it?"

"Zilch. Can I confiscate your phone?"

"No. I'm on call two nights a week. Plus, patients who need to can contact me directly. Everyone said I was nuts, but patients rarely abuse the privilege."

Wills pressed his lower lip with upper teeth. He ran a hand across both cheeks. "I'll get a warrant for the phone. County will provide you a replacement you can download everything into. We'll want to keep the original."

"So you don't think his basically confessing has much value?"

"It's illegal in California to record a conversation without the other party's knowledge," Wills said.

"Not if it's part of a public meeting. Or if I recorded it to obtain evidence of a felony."

Wills shook his head. "That's dicey. A public meeting? No third-party voices are heard. Number two, any value of the recording in court is weakened by you drawing blood. His attorney would say fear of more violence caused Moran to say what he thought you wanted him to say. But that's not my department. And keep in mind you don't have a department. I think we're done. Thank you for bringing this to my attention."

I got up from the awful chair. Mimicking Wills, I said, "I think you're hiding something."

This broke some ice. Wills even smiled. "At least I admit it," he said. His smile grew. "Can you show yourself out?"

It was becoming a long day and that, too, reminded me of being on the hunt for Sherman Investigations. A practice of never letting up until I prevailed, born on basketball courts, still resided in me. It had been dormant for a handful of years. I welcomed its reappearance. Worried I'd driven away a second woman I loved, feeling the old loneliness creeping back in, I plowed onward. I was too jacked up to go sit alone in my house without halls.

From Santa Rosa I took River Road thirty miles due west. Then it was the climbing of Bishop's Grade to Ridge Road, and on to Wathor Mountain Road. The pavement narrowed as dusk became night.

I parked at the Finnegans' gate, lowered the window and pressed the horn. It sounded like an invasion. *Good*, I thought. The Finnegans had to already be on edge. Carbone had warned them to close their poaching operation. Rick and Carbone were dead. I honked a few more times. I looked forward to giving the people I figured had drugged me a hard time. I looked forward to making them sweat.

Engine sounds grew closer. I took my red switchblade from the glove box and got out of the car with it and a flashlight in hand. The knife went into a back pocket. I stepped beside the tall wood gate, to the barbed wire fence, and waved the flashlight overhead. The Simpkins Furniture Delivery and Installation van appeared, which struck me as amusing considering how many miles I'd driven it. Did the Finnegans know I'd been a courier? Probably, be it by way of Moran or De Laat, or both. The van stopped. Air wavered in front of its headlights. Joan stayed behind the steering wheel. Jim climbed out, carrying a flashlight of his own. He wore a large, hooded sweatshirt, maybe gray. Jim advanced with his head down. He reached the other side of the fence.

"What do you want?"

"I'm interested in psychedelics. You have any?"

I caught a glance of Jim's snotty grin. He turned toward the van. He drew a hand across his Adam's apple. The van's engine was turned off, then its lights.

"Did you hear that?" Jim called. "The doctor guy wants to buy drugs."

Joan got out of the van. With the van's engine turned off, the shutting of its door sounded extra loud out there.

"He came to the wrong place," Joan said. She walked with her arms folded in front of her. She watched her footsteps in the darkness, careful not to trip, and stopped next to Jim.

"Sorry," I said. "I meant to say I came for poached venison."

Jim shined the light at me. "I don't know what you're talking about."

Joan said. "What did you think of the Session? Your first, right?"

"Interesting. But not as interesting as venison. Or abalone. Or sea turtles. You get the idea."

Jim said, "And you get the fuck out of here. You're trespassing."

I couldn't see either of their faces. They did not sound stoned.

"After he tells us the real reason he came," Joan said.

"In a way, Mayor Carbone sent me."

"Don't joke about it," said Joan. "His drowning was a heartbreaker."

Joan's tone lopped off some of the conversation's angry tenor. We were quiet. Metal cooling, the van's engine made a ticking sound.

"We agree," I said. "And Mayor Carbone would want you to

know you should clear out everything fast. The police could show up as early as tomorrow. That's what I was told."

I misled in hopes of causing them to act rashly and make some kind of mistake.

"Just a minute," Joan said. She grabbed Jim by an elbow, and they headed for the van. "Don't leave. Okay?"

Leaving hadn't entered my mind. The van's front doors opened, shut loudly. I transferred the six-inch switchblade to my better coordinated half hand.

A couple of minutes later, the Finnegans followed Jim's flashlight across grass. I tried to see if anything else was in their hands. They reached the steel fence. Joan flashed the peace sign to me.

"Look," she said. "We had no idea who you were at Homer's. Then you're at the hospital with Rick. It wigged us out."

Jim said, "It was just an easy hundred bucks. We scrounge for everything we can, to keep on keeping on. All we knew was to look for your hand. We were told the whole thing was a joke, on a friend. You got a problem with it, talk to Odin."

"I will. For now, let's move on from that. What's important now is I was told things that mean you better act quickly."

"Mayor Carbone said we have until August first," Jim said.

"He told me that, too. The day before he was found dead on Sunset Beach. Trust me, things have changed."

Jim thrust his face to inches from the fence. "How do we know this isn't some kind of setup? How do we know what you say isn't crap?"

"I guess you don't. Hear me out, and I'll leave."

Jim's voice rose. "Make it fast. You're basically threatening us.

I'm losing my patience."

"I've discovered Moran drove the car that killed Mystery Woman. If you know that, you should give it up before the cops come. Moran's going down. Withholding evidence will only make matters worse for you if you have to deal with the police."

"We don't know shit about that woman getting hit," Jim said.

Joan said, "Let him talk."

The night was cooling fast.

I said, "Don't give up anything else. Rick's dead. It may not have been an accident. If you know anything, save it for a lawyer to use. Get a good one, because Moran will sell you out, and whoever else he can pin blame on. Don't talk to anybody involved. Don't answer texts or calls. They're the same as a paper trail."

"Why the hell," Jim said, "would you help us and not screw us?"

"Because Mayor Carbone wanted to help you. Because my focus is on a killer. Poaching is between you and the police."

This time it was Jim, not Joan, who seized an elbow. "He's trying to get us to turn against each other. He's out to get us. Know it."

Jim led Joan to the van. Its doors opened, then slammed. Headlights and the engine went on. The van bounced when turning around. As it headed into darkness a shadowy arm rose out from the passenger-side window.

Jim Finnegan flipped me the bird.

Thirty-one

Not another car was seen all the way down the long descent of Wathor Mountain Road. The Subaru's headlights reached far into the woods. On Ridge Road a Jeep passed going in the opposite direction, followed by a car. Their lights were circular beams moving through blackness. Little Tibetan prayer flags were still displayed at the 4600-address marker.

I wondered what Inez was doing.

Fifteen minutes later, descending a favored stretch of Bishop's Grade, there was not a house to be seen. Lights showed in my rear-view mirror. They became brighter. Looking down, I saw I was going under the speed limit. In the rear-view mirror the headlights came at me well above the speed limit. As they neared, the vehicle shimmied. High beams shot white lights. In the side-view mirror I saw it was a van. No way was I going to pull over. Not out there. I hit the gas.

It was half a dozen miles to coastal Highway One, where there would be enough traffic to deter an angry Finnegan, I assumed Jim, from trying anything. Jim used guns to poach deer and game birds. I wasn't about to let him poach me.

While glancing again in the rear-view mirror, the road

curved. Tires screeched and spit gravel. I barely made the turn. The van spurted ahead, getting closer. The road suddenly dipped and curved. I skidded and battled the steering wheel. The road straightened. To both sides the land opened up.

I continued down Bishop's Grade. No headlights followed me. At an old ranching road blocked by a locked gate, I stopped. No vehicle came down the hill. There hadn't been a place to turn around where I last saw the van. Finnegan might have lost control and crashed. I turned around and headed back up. At reaching the stretch where the van was last seen behind me, I turned on the high beams. Ahead, to the right, was another ranch road blocked by a gate. The gate had a No Hunting sign on it and looked like it hadn't been opened in a generation. I parked, took my flashlight and switchblade, and walked downhill on the other side of the road. I came to where something had carved a path through brush; I walked on stripped branches. Picking my way along, ahead, on its side, I saw the van. One headlight still on, the engine dead, its front end had bashed into a large fir tree. A check of my phone showed ample reception.

"Over here. I'm over here."

The squeaky voice of a man in pain.

"Where are you?"

"Behind the van."

I swept the light over the ground. Thirty feet away a body was on its back, sprawled on crushed brush.

"Are you armed? If you want help, tell me the truth."

"What are you talking about, armed?"

"Odin?"

"Who in the hell do you think I am?"

All fear vanished. I pushed my way through brush toward the sprawled body. My breaths spread steam. The flashlight beam found a bald head. I pointed the light at the van and barely made out *Odin's Antiques* amidst fresh scratches and snapped branches. At reaching Odin I stood beside him. The brush elevated him to about a bed's height.

"Are you bleeding?"

"No." Odin grunted in pain. "My legs are trashed. I think both broken. I can only crawl. Couldn't make it to the road."

I slowly ran the light down his body. Below the knees his legs splayed at unusual angles.

"Follow my finger with your eyes."

Odin did so.

"Call 9-1-1," he said. "My phone's somewhere in the van. Couldn't find it, so crawled out."

"Count to twenty by fours, then back to zero."

"Goddamn it! Get some help."

"Count by fours, so I know your mind's working okay."

Odin swore and swiftly counted by fours to twenty and back. "My legs hurt like hell. It's—get me out of here."

I was careful not to touch him. "I'll be right back."

Odin's torso lifted off the bed-like mass of brush he was on. "What?"

"My car's up the road, with my medical bag."

"Call 9-1-1."

"No reception." I was going to talk with Odin. Just the two of us. "This will take a few."

I made my way to Bishop's Grade and jogged to the car, reached behind the driver's seat and pulled out the black bag.

I considered various options. Then opened the bag, withdrew a set of surgical gloves, closed and dropped the medical bag on the backseat. I jogged down the road and worked my way through brush. My body moving through brush announced my arrival.

"What took you so long? This hurts, man."

I sat in a small clearing a ways behind Odin. He craned his neck, trying to see me. I didn't shine light in his direction. Surrounded by forest, in near total darkness I said, "Let's talk."

"Talk? Get me out of here."

"Why were you chasing me?"

Odin twisted his neck again. "Goddamn it, give me a pain killer or something."

"What brought on the chase? You could've killed me."

Odin spewed profanities. He kicked his legs in frustration, which caused him to yell in pain. Then all was quiet except Odin's pained breathing, which sent steam straight up.

I waited for his answer. Odin wasn't in immediate danger. I was in no hurry.

"Look," Odin said. "I'm up at Mr. Moran's. He gets a call, leaves the room. When he comes back, he says if I scare the hell out of you, my delivery debts are canceled. Wiped out if I scare you enough you stay out of his life."

"What were you doing up there?"

"He offered me work. The twins left. Get this. They emptied the house of cash, and just up and left. Mr. Moran said he'd hire me to do some of their stuff."

"Okay. Now, Rick Fulton. How did he end up driving off a road he drove all the time?"

Again, Odin's body twisted, trying to see me. "I don't know anything about Fulton. Swear to god."

"How did Mayor Carbone die?"

"I only know what the papers say. Drowned himself rather than face what he'd let go on for years. Couldn't take the public shame."

"Do you believe it?"

Odin lifted his head, turned it some to the side. "I've told you what I know. Now do your job and go get some help."

I stood, and flicked twigs and leaves off my jeans. "I'm not able to do that."

"What? Head for Jenner. Soon as reception hits, call 9-1-1."

"If I call, I'll have to tell the police you tried to run me off the road. How else would I know you crashed? Their questions might lead to telling them you paid me to deliver illegal food. Then we're both nailed. You get it? It's in your best interest to tell the police you lost control going down the grade. A top-heavy van—hey, I'm doing you a favor."

"The hell you are."

"When I find your phone and hand it to you, you'll realize this is best."

Odin shouted, "You bastard! You said there's no reception."

"Listen. Do you want to, for example, explain to me about paying a hundred bucks to get me drugged, or do you want me to find your phone?"

"Get the phone and get the hell out of here."

"Now we're on the same page."

With the surgical gloves on, I went to the crashed van. The phone had been thrown behind the driver's seat. I found it when opening the lower—because it was on its side—van back door. Its location made me think Odin had been talking on the phone when he'd lost control and crashed. That didn't worry me. He certainly hadn't been talking to his mother or a priest.

I made sure Odin held the phone securely in both hands before heading through crackling, dark woods. He didn't waste breath on yelling more profanities. It would take more than hour for an ambulance to reach him. By then I'd be close to home.

As to who had phoned Moran, it had to be Jim or Joan Finnegan, shortly after they drove off. They probably thought they were helping Moran and repeated the lie I'd told that the police would soon pounce. And hopefully, Odin would report to Moran about me not calling the authorities, and leaving him with his phone at the crash scene. That would get Moran wondering what I was up to, which might set in motion an unforced error on his part. The truth was, there was no plan. I was fishing blind.

Thirty-two

With no call from the police by noon Sunday, I figured Odin had claimed he'd lost control speeding down Bishop's Grade. Restless, I packed food and water, drove to Dutton Beach and ran sprints until I practically dropped.

I drove to SunSpot and hiked to Edwina's. The blue tarp, while still strung, sagged across the top. I fiddled with how it was hooked onto the bark, brushed off fallen redwood needles, and entered. I'd brought the book *Wild Oats in Eden*. I ate and read and wondered what Inez was doing. After finishing the book, I drove home.

When reaching in a pocket for the door key, footsteps pounded down the driveway. I spun around. Jim Finnegan sprang up two concrete stairs to the porch. His eyes were as wild as Rick Fulton's the day Rick showed up at Yates Health with Kim. Jim's right arm slashed half a circle, ripping a knife across my stomach.

As his arm withdrew, readying for another strike, I shoved him—hard—backwards. He tripped on the concrete step and fell with me on top of him. I grabbed his wrist, slammed it against pavement. The knife clattered away. My hands went to Jim's throat. Adrenaline in the driver's seat, I squeezed his windpipe, jamming both thumbs in deep. He gagged. I squeezed and blocked all air until he quit struggling, and then I climbed off.

I threw the knife past the driveway into weeds. Jim held his throat and made desperate-sounding gurgles. I stomped him from the side, three times. It brought a shuddering of Jim's body, and high-pitched wailing.

"You move," I said, "I'll break your neck."

Jim was in no condition to move. His hands stayed at this throat.

I pulled out my phone, dialed 9-1-1, said I'd been attacked and gave the address. "It's the house in back."

Looking over, I saw blood speckled on Jim's shirt. I looked down. The bottom of my T-shirt was dripping blood. To the phone I said, "Could you tell them to hurry?"

I noted the sky was cloudless. A power mower buzzed in someone's backyard down the block. It seemed a nice sound. I went weak in the knees, and gradually, collapsed. I pressed hands into the now crimson bloody T-shirt, onto the cut, to slow bleeding. It didn't hurt as badly as you'd think.

I looked to the other prone body. "What the hell's wrong with you? I've been withholding info from the police. Giving you a chance."

Between half gagging breaths, Jim got out, "Mr. Moran told me what you're up to." Jim appeared dazed, like he was unsure of where he was. "If he gives you twenty grand, you'll go to the cops, blame everything on me and Joan, and keep you two out of it. He said if I don't make you shut up, we'll go to jail."

My eyes closed. I rested my head on the asphalt driveway. The last thing I remember was saying, "You stupid ass. Moran just got you in big trouble."

A purring sound, like the hummingbirds, if they were indeed hummingbirds, that flitted around the bushes in the garden at SunSpot. Slowly, things came into focus. A hospital room. Inez, looking distraught.

"Hello," she said.

I tried to think straight. "How did you know?"

"In the ambulance you kept asking them to call me."

"You came."

"Of course I came."

Inez looped her brown purse overhead, set it aside and took a seat. Behind her a female nurse stood watch. She wore a pale blue face mask. They had me high on something. It felt like I was a balloon sailing around the room with the air rushing out. To keep a steady view of Inez was not possible.

The nurse stepped forward. "Dr. Arne said five minutes. I let it go until you saw him wake up. So. You know?"

Inez touched the nurse on her shoulder. "Thank you." To me, she said, "I'll be here in the morning."

"Where am I?"

"Memorial Hospital."

"Really?"

"Really. He got a pretty good slice of your stomach, but didn't hit any organs.

The nurse said, "Inez."

"I know."

Inez scooted past the nurse, kissed me on a cheek and left the room. As doped up as they had me, everything seemed to happen in a dream I watched unspool in front of me.

The nurse straightened blankets, adjusted the pillow behind my head.

I said, "Have you ever thought maybe everything's a dream? That nothing's really real?"

The nurse smiled. "Now, like doctor said, keep your hands away from your stomach. If you can't help yourself," she said, and pointed bedside, "press this button. This one here. You see it?"

In the morning, like when awakening the night before, the first thing I saw was Inez's face. She squeezed my hand.

"How do you feel?"

"Like somebody knifed me."

Dr. Arne strode into the room. As tall as my six-feet-three, like a lot of tall people, out of habit, he stooped forward a bit to make better eye contact with people. His hair was a white mop. He more resembled a wily college professor than a medical doctor. Arne asked Inez to wait in the hall while he examined me, and yanked the thin beige curtain around the bed.

My hospital gown was lifted; I held it chest high.

"You're lucky your attacker didn't know what he was doing. He went across the gut instead of straight in." Arne, sixties, had keen eyes. "Do you think you can deal with the pain without medication?"

"Yes."

"Good. We'll let it hurt. That will help you keep your hands off the sutures."

"I feel fine. Can you release me now?"

Arne chuckled. "Ms. Vasquez warned me you're a handful. I'll return about three this afternoon, administer a fresh dressing, see how you're doing. If you're calmer than you are now, you can sign yourself out under your own care. I'll leave instructions to that effect." Arne stood, tugged the cloth curtain around, to re-open it. "I'm assuming you'll arrange for someone to drive you."

Inez came back into the room, which was a single because the police had been involved and might return for questioning. She plucked a clear plastic baggy from her purse. In it were my wallet, phone and keys. She dropped the keys into her purse, and set the wallet and phone on the bedside table.

"Call me," Inez said, "when Dr. Arne says you can go. I'll pick up something for you to wear."

I looked at the wallet and phone. "They gave you those?"

"I had to be sure you wouldn't wake up and start calling people. See what you could find out about the Finnegans." Inez kissed me on the mouth. She whispered, "When they told me you'd been stabbed, I almost had a heart attack."

As soon as Inez left, I called attorney Debra Morehouse. Her assistant forwarded me to voice mail. I said Frank Carbone had mentioned her as a good lawyer. Said I needed representation and, in a shorthanded way, described what I'd been involved in.

While searching online for an article about Odin being found in the woods, Lieutenant Wills called. "I'm in another part of the building. Just interviewed Jim Finnegan. I'm hoping you'll be able to clarify a few—"

I cut him off. "Now I do need a lawyer. Won't say anything until I've had a chance to meet with her. Just so you know."

"I'll be damned." I pictured Wills brushing his mustache, dark brown eyes intent on an open notebook. "I think you're actually going to cooperate. By the way, we have the knife. I'm sure it'll have Finnegan's DNA all over it."

I told Wills I'd contact him as soon as I'd spoken with Morehouse.

"Morehouse will make the contact. She isn't going to let you say a word to me unless she's present. Till then."

Wills disconnected.

Considering the circumstances, I felt pretty good. And lucky. Inez was coming to take me home in the afternoon. Moran's life was bound to go downhill fast. Finnegan's, too. Searching the *Daily Democrat's* Facebook page, its top posting was Appleton Antique Dealer in Solo Crash. It mentioned that Odin had been transported to the U.C. Medical Center in San Francisco, where a specialist would work on his broken legs. The article reported they had both suffered compound fractures. I had to admit that Odin was one tough antique salesman and crook.

I drifted in and out of sleep between searching for more Odin information and anything about Moran, the Finnegans or Carbone. Inez arrived with a shirt, jeans, underwear and socks. My tennis shoes had blood spots on them but were dry. At reaching the house without halls, Inez said she had to get back to close Yates Health, and that she'd swing by later with dinner.

Attorney Morehouse called. She was no-nonsense and easy going at the same time. I told her everything, from Odin's first suggestion to me about driving the van to raise money for the clinic, the stabbing of the night before, and everything in between except Edwina's spectral lineage.

"That's quite a story."

"Will you represent me?"

"You think I'm going to pass this one up? Since you're housebound, I'll come your way. Tomorrow, two o'clock? You'll need to sign some papers. Don't talk to anyone else about this."

Thirty-three

Shannon called at eleven the next morning. His voice seemed to crunch the words as they flew. "Went up to paint today."

"You agreed to stay away."

"Hey, I been curious. Going every chance I get. Today I'm up giving the rafters a new color. Moran comes outside. He's got a small suitcase in each hand. He runs to the Expedition and he's out of there. I drop everything and follow. But give him a big lead. At Ridge Road, I figure to the coast. Long and short, I followed him to Santa Rosa. He just got on 101 North. You know, like for the airport. I been holding back on calling in case it was a false alarm."

Shannon's excitement fed mine. I jumped up from the couch. Like lit matches, a tearing sensation burned at the stitches. "Don't let him see you."

"I know what I'm doing."

"Park at the back end of the rental lot. Less chance he'll see your truck. Find his car, watch it. I'm calling the cops and coming in. He's got to check in well before takeoff."

"What should I do till you get here?"

"If the police arrive, wave them down. Tell them the person

who hit Mystery Woman is flying away. Describe and name him."

"You think Mor—"

"Yes. Say that. For now, use your phone to find next departure times and destinations."

It was twenty-five minutes from my place to the Sonoma County Airport. On the way I left a message on Lieutenant Wills' phone and called the main line for the sheriff's department. The man answering blew me off until I rattled off Will's cell number and told him I was going to the airport to stop a killer from flying away. That gained his attention.

I exited Highway 101 at Airport Boulevard, went left, crossed train tracks, and soon reached the airport's small parking lot. Circling it took less than thirty seconds. I snatched a ticket from the machine, parked in the first open slot and climbed out into summer heat. Shannon stood at the edge of the rental lot, watching the black Expedition.

He saw me running toward him, pointed to the terminal and called, "Next flight's to L.A. They'll be boarding by now."

The small lot was easy to pass through. I crossed the street to the terminal entrance, stopped at facing high walls of glass, took a breath to slow myself, and entered. With one main hallway leading to the boarding gates, it wasn't difficult to know where to look. I hid behind a wide, square, off-white column.

Moran sat in a row of otherwise empty chairs, against a wall near the restrooms. Over the public address system came a last call for the flight to Los Angeles. Moran headed for the main hall carrying two suitcases small enough for carry-on. From my position I looked straight into it. A metal detector and conveyor belt were at the near end. Two security guards stood beyond the metal detector. Their badges shined, their eyes moved about. Their demeanor was not laid back.

Wills must have made a quick phone call.

Moran glided ahead, turned right, and slowed as his gaze took in the security guards. He casually left the airport through a side exit. There was only one way to go from there. A narrow cement path led to the front of the terminal. Cars arrived, people clambered out. A yellow taxi waited curbside; smoke puffed from its tailpipe. Moran got to the road before I did. He maneuvered between traffic like a kayak running rapids. I took off—a horn blared—heading for the black Expedition roughly fifty yards away. Moran cut the distance in half. Shannon rushed from the rental lot, his thick frame galloping toward the Expedition, right fist raised in a warning.

Moran saw Shannon, dropped the suitcase in his right hand and cut left. He wore all black. His legs pumped wildly. He reached Airport Boulevard. He ran hard.

It was a foot race. A straight line on a sidewalk past businesses. We crossed one side street. No cars or buildings impeded us. Moran was fast. I was faster. I told myself to ignore the tearing and pain in my middle, to focus on catching saintly Edwina's killer.

Ahead, three sets of flashing lights raced toward us. Two were atop police cars, the third set, smaller, just two lights, was perched on the dashboard of a white civilian SUV. Vehicles pulled over. Red and blue lights whizzed past them. No sirens wailed. By then I was close enough to hear the snapping of Moran's footsteps on the sidewalk.

I roared and gave chase with every bit of strength I had.

And dove and tackled him from behind. The brown suitcase flew, then skidded ahead on the sidewalk. I kept Moran on his stomach by jamming a knee in the middle of his back and yanking both arms up behind him. I was so jacked up I didn't smell peaches.

Moran's legs kicked frantically.

Shannon arrived.

"Get his legs!"

Shannon, wheezing, plopped his 230 pounds on Moran's calves. The fleeing man no longer moved. Shannon broke into a coughing fit.

The police vehicles crossed lanes and stopped at odd angles to the sidewalk. Wills got out of the SUV and ran in our direction. Two uniformed policemen did the same. They drew pistols.

Wills arrived first. "You two, get off him."

I let go, stumbled off, pressed hands to my stomach.

Shannon got up. He delivered me a triumphant, if gasping nod. "Got him." Then his splotchy red face fell into a grimace. "Woodrow. You're bleeding."

Wills pointed to a crisp green lawn with an elevated sign that read Wright Engineered Plastics. "Over there. Both of you."

We stepped that way and sat on the grass. I was drenched in sweat. Torn stitches seemed to scrape me from inside, and the number of lit matches that seemed to burn there had increased considerably.

Wills said, "Are you injured, Mr. Moran? Do you have need of an ambulance?"

Moran didn't say anything. He remained face down.

Shannon said, "The guy that's injured is over here. Get him to a hospital."

Wills waved a finger at Shannon. "You speak when spoken to." He turned to the man face down on the sidewalk. "Did these men assault you?"

No answer.

The drawn guns were holstered. Traffic slowed, as gawkers took in the scene. The two uniformed officers watched all this. Behind them red and blue lights danced.

Wills stood over Moran. "This is an opportunity to tell us what happened."

Moran, still on the ground, turned away from Wills like a petulant child.

"Okay. If that's how you want to play it." Wills spoke to the elder of the two deputies. "Deputy Thomsen, take Dr. Taylor to emergency. Stay with him until he is signed in and under a doctor's care. Dr. Taylor, have your attorney call me first thing in the morning."

"Fair enough."

Wills removed Moran's wallet from a back pocket of his now-scuffed black jeans. He didn't bother opening it. He handed it to the younger officer. "Deputy August, Moran's yours. You cuff him and do the arrest. Call me after the emergency room doc examines him. Put the doctor on the phone even if he says he's too busy. I'll give you further instructions at that time. And don't forget the suitcase over there. Now, Lunge."

"Yes, sir," Shannon said.

"Do you have a vehicle here?"

"Yes."

"You can go straight home. Be at my sheriff's department office at nine a.m. Will you be able to find it?"

Shannon said he'd be there.

Wills said, "I was called away from my five-year-old daughter's birthday party. She only turns five once." He angrily stepped toward me. "Taylor, you're a pain in the ass." Wills turned to the two uniformed officers. He threw up his hands and shot them a fiery look. "I got an idea. How about if you men start earning your salaries?"

After the lower stomach was numbed, and a patch of stitches was replaced, I was released from the hospital. The damage from sprinting and grappling with Moran had torn out two of four inches of stitches crossing my lower stomach. I hailed an Uber, was driven to the airport, picked up my car and, breaking a promise made to the emergency room doctor, drove myself home. The numbing agent wore off. It was replaced by half a bottle of a local pinot noir. Hell yes I was celebrating.

For the second evening in a row, Inez brought dinner. I could tell she hadn't heard anything about what happened at the airport, because she smiled brightly as she closed the door behind her with a foot.

"How'd your day go?"

I laughed so hard the stitches felt like they might burst through the skin. Inez set a bag of food on the teak table and came to me with a grave look twisting her face. She sat on the plum-colored chair across from me. I forced myself to squelch the laughter.

"What in the world's so funny?"

I told Inez about Shannon's call, and what happened after I met him at the airport. Her expression stayed grave the whole time. Her eyes squinched closed when I told her about the new stitches.

Inez got up, went to the big square window and looked out at the unkempt apple orchard. "You're not exactly giving me confidence about us."

"Moran drove the car that killed Mystery Lady. I got his confession recorded. Jim Finnegan has been illegally shooting deer and game birds. Now he's busted. Odin De Laat got what he deserved. I'll tell you all about it if you promise not to walk out."

Inez's hands rested on the kitchen counter. She continued to look out the window. "Tell me about it over dinner. I'm hungry."

When I finished telling Inez everything, we'd long finished eating. The big question for me was whether Inez would tell me to go to hell and leave or tell me to go to hell and stay.

"I'm pissed," Inez said. "You push everything to extremes. You're reckless. Can you handle taking care of yourself?"

"Of course."

"Good, because I'm out of here."

There was no kiss goodbye.

I spent most of the night awake, rehearsing justifications for my actions.

In the morning, Shannon called. "I got raked over coals by that Wills cop. For like an hour."

"What did you tell him?"

"The truth, including it was me who took the bumper pictures. Once you start with lies, you can't keep 'em straight. I don't want no trouble."

"You're a wise man."

"Hey, Doc. I didn't know about what that scumbag did, with the knife. You gonna be okay?"

"Not to worry. He missed the important parts."

"I'll check in tomorrow. I'm late for a job out on Westside Road."

Attorney Morehouse and I met at our scheduled two p.m. She was petite, quick of mind and quick in movements. A real pro. She described her morning phone conversation with Lieutenant Wills as a friendly chat.

"How much trouble am I in?"

"Let's not approach it from that angle."

"I guess it's a lot of trouble."

"We have things to work with. For example, the D.A.'s office will press charges against Finnegan, which they'll leverage to get Finnegan to flip on Moran. Once Finnegan talks about how Moran sent him to hurt you, potentially kill you, we use that against any assault charges Moran might file against you and Shannon. Who I'll contact and suggest I represent. In light of Moran's crimes, I'm not worried about the recording potentially not being legal. And so on. In the short term, you stay under the radar while these people start throwing each other under the bus. I mean it. Don't get curious and start sniffing around."

"How long do you think it will take for all this to play out?"

"It depends on the direction the D.A.'s office takes. If things go your way, I estimate two years. Maybe three."

Thirty-four

For a few days life was a combination of media people hounding me, and depositions, at my place, with Morehouse who provided chairs, a court reporter, and Assistant District Attorney Lynn Palmberg. At first Palmberg was put off by the county's allowing questioning of me while couch bound at home, but in the end seemed to enjoy the informality. She asked what seemed about a thousand questions. Morehouse tapped the teak dining table—finally put to use—whenever I was to take the fifth. Her knuckles must have become exceptionally sore.

Moran was charged with a multitude of crimes. Jim Finnegan, who by illegally killing animals and leaving evidence around in the form of pelts, antlers and bones, would likely end up with jail time. He was chivalrous, claiming Joan knew nothing about it. Joan swore to that, adding that she'd never in her life fired a gun. I didn't know what went on with Kim, but the police couldn't just leave her out of it. As to Bam and Sam, they had simply disappeared with an unknown amount of Moran's cash.

Odin's name didn't appear in the press again, and I didn't initiate inquiries about him.

All week, after work Inez swung by with dinner, turning away from cameras and wading through women and men in suits shoving microphones at her. She'd cooled off, with an emphasis on being chilly. We were taking things slow, feeling each other out. Friday night, after the media circus left, we moved to Inez's house to throw them off. I settled in on the futon couch in the living room.

"I miss Bianca."

"She asks about you on the phone."

I tugged the bottom of my T-shirt. "What do we tell her about this?"

"As little as possible. I want to let her be a kid."

"How would you feel about me staying here when Bianca comes back? I want to help with the single parent situation. You both mean more to me than anything else."

The expression on Inez's face changed, though I couldn't read into it. The stakes—what would become of our love—heightened right then. Nothing less than my chance at having a good life was on the line.

"Well," Inez said, "now look who wants to talk about feelings." She left her chair, gave my knee a rap. "Let's do the one day at a time thing."

Inez said goodnight. I kept my mouth shut and pulled a blanket over myself.

In the morning, Dale called. "Chris wants to know if you can confirm you'll be available when principal photography begins, in fifteen days. My names feed shows you took a meeting with a knife."

"It won't be a problem."

"That's good news. We'll be in touch."

Not one question about getting stabbed. The show must go on!

Moran was the object of more attention than I. The sixty-five hundred dollars in traveler's checks found in his small suitcase drew internet comments, as did the plane tickets he'd purchased: The one to Los Angeles, and another, a one-way flight to Belize. Speculation was that when making fast money, in his Silicon Valley days, Moran had stashed chunks of it in a secret Belize bank account.

Things began to settle down. I called Sheriff Niles. After hellos, I asked, "Is there any evidence showing Carbone had actually been in the boat found at Oberti Point?"

Niles spoke in his usual affable tone. "You know I can't answer that."

"In case that's a no, let me speculate a little. What if Carbone was never in the stolen boat? What if two huge tough guys who worked for Moran—who have disappeared—took Frank in another boat owned by a fellow named Jim Finnegan? What if one grabbed Frank by his uniform and chucked him overboard, not thinking he'd wash to shore? Then they steal and crash the boat from Timber Cove to make it look like a suicide. What if you contacted Sonoma County police, and suggest they try for DNA samples on Finnegan's boat?"

"You call that a little speculation?" Niles asked.

"I misspoke. But what do you think?"

"I think," Niles began, then ceased speaking for perhaps half a minute that seemed longer. "What I think is, you need to decide what you really want in life. What you want in the big picture. Pursue it with all you got. Everything else is just noise."

We said goodbyes. I looked around Inez's cozy house, a house filled with love, and thought about what Niles had said. For the rest of the day I thought about what Niles had said.

That night I told Inez I was done with secrets, and there was something I needed to show her. Early Sunday morning, before any media surmised we were at her place, Inez drove us to SunSpot. Nervous about what I was about to tell her, stomach stinging from walking on steep, uneven terrain, I pressed a hand on the stitches as we descended. Inez and I walked to the thicket tunnel. She made no small talk. Crawling through the tunnel was painful. My mood lifted as we walked among virgin redwood trees. We approached the gloaming blue tarp. Inez gave me a questioning look.

I unhooked the tarp, and pulled it aside. "After you."

Inez ducked and entered. "So, this is where Mystery Woman lived."

I followed and shined a flashlight throughout the neatly organized tree abode. "Her name was Edwina. We shared special time here."

Inez's hands combed back through her dark hair. "You said you never even touched her."

"I didn't. But I need to tell you about her. She was something that's hard to explain."

We sat on the tan blankets. I turned off the flashlight. I talked about Edwina, omitting nothing. It came out easily, naturally. After finishing, I felt relieved. I'd dropped the considerable weight of a months-long burden.

Inez said, "Let's lie down and be quiet for a while."

On my side, back-to-back with Inez, I felt connected with everything in that hollowed-out place formed by lightning. "Feel how warm it is? It's always warm in here, day or night."

No response.

"You just have to let it in."

"It's weird you keep coming here, but that's not what worries me. At least not what worries me most." Inez placed a hand on my hip. "Would you consider seeing someone about this ghost stuff? It's not real."

"Let's go back to being quiet. You'll feel it. I promise it will reach you."

I believed Inez would eventually feel what I did when inside Edwina's tiny abode. The questions provoked by the drugging had, of late, been replaced by wondering what Edwina's appearance in my life meant. Surely it wasn't an accident our paths had crossed, as it surely wasn't an accident Kim showed up in my life on the day she chopped off halves of two fingers.

Outside, from downhill, came footsteps. They weren't loud but they sounded clearly enough you could tell they were coming in our direction. Inez and I sat up. No person or animal was visible, though our field of vision was limited. The footsteps stopped at what sounded like right in front of the tree trunk opening.

A single puff of wind enhanced the powerful scent of a redwood forest.

Inez gripped my arm. She whispered, "What is it?"

"I don't know."

Edwina's calming voice filled the hollowed tree base. "Everything is okay."

The footsteps retreated. I clambered outside, still hearing footsteps and seeing nothing but redwood trees and the shaded spaces between them.

Inez came out. She pointed toward the footsteps sounds. She shook her head, clearly astonished. "We don't tell anybody about this. Not a soul."

"Not a single soul," I said.

About the Author

Scott Lipanovich's stories have appeared in *Ireland's Fish Story Prize*, *The Seattle Review*, *Crosscurrents*, *Defiant Scribe*, *Abiko* (Japan), *Wild Duck Review*, *Ridge Review*, *Gold and Treasure Hunter Magazine*, *Summerfield Journal*, and several anthologies. In film, he has worked with two Academy Award winners and two multiple Emmy-winning producers.

Scott is the author of the Jeff Taylor Mysteries, *The Lost Coast* (July 2021), *The Golden Ceiling* (July 2022), *Sky Lake* (July 2023), and *West County* (July 2025). He lives in Santa Rosa, California.

If you enjoyed this book,
please consider writing a review
and sharing it with other readers.

Thank you,
Encircle Publications

For news about more exciting new fiction, join us at:

Facebook: www.facebook.com/encirclepub

Instagram: www.instagram.com/encirclepublications